The Silent Boy

The Silent Boy

LOIS LOWRY

Houghton Mifflin Company Boston 2003

Walter Lorraine Books

Walter Lorraine (wr) Books

www.houghtonmifflinbooks.com

Library of Congress Cataloging-in-Publication Data

Lowry, Lois.
 The silent boy / Lois Lowry.
  p. cm.
Summary: Katy, the precocious ten-year-old daughter of the
 town doctor, befriends a retarded boy.
 ISBN 0-618-28231-9
 [1. People with mental disabilities—Fiction. 2. Babies—Fiction. 3.
Brothers and sisters—Fiction. 4. Unmarried mothers—Fiction.] I.
Title.
 PZ7.L9673 To 2003
 [Fic]—dc21
                                                    2002009072

Printed in the United States of America
VB 10 9 8 7 6 5 4 3 2 1

Acknowledgments

Few things give me more pleasure than looking at photographs. To glimpse other lives, caught and captured in moments that live on long after the circumstances of the moment have passed, makes me shiver with imagination.

All of the people in these photographs are real people. Some of them were people I knew and loved. One is my own mother.

Others are strangers. But people who knew them have generously allowed me to use them to illustrate this story.

In particular I want to thank Betty Landis Carson, who sent me some photos from her own family collection; and Rex and Phyllis Reynolds Naylor, who did as well.

But there is no way to thank the people whose family photographs ended up in the New Hampshire antique store where I found them. I find myself wondering about those beautiful children, those wide-eyed young girls, those sturdy young men—all of them captured by a camera in the early part of the century when cameras were still a novelty. Someone must have treasured their pictures once. Someone knew their names and what their stories were.

Now I have turned them into fiction. I can only hope that they wouldn't mind.

Lois Lowry
Cambridge, Massachusetts
March 2002

Contents

PROLOGUE: JUNE 1987

I am a very old woman now. My great-grand-children—who call me Docky, a name my youngest patients gave me years ago—ask me to tell them stories, and I make up tales about talking pigs with pink hair ribbons on their curly tails, or monkeys who wear vests and carry canes. I am as good at foolishness as I once was in the operating room.

If I tried to tell them this story, the one I am about to set down here, their parents would send me warning looks over the heads of the children. *Don't*, the looks would say. *Stop.*

1

Meaning, too depressing. Too complicated. Too long ago.

So when they come to me—young Austin, named for his great-grandfather; the twins, Sam and Zoe; merry-eyed Lily, adopted from China; and solemn Katharine, who has my name but insists on it whole, never Katy, as I once was, or Kate, as I am now—when they come and ask me to tell them stories, I never tell them this one.

It is not really a story for children, though it is about a child.

But someday one of them will point from a car window toward a huge stone building with boarded windows set in an empty, unlandscaped field at the west side of town and ask, "What's that?" Perhaps they will see, through untrimmed ivy on the stone wall surrounding the field, the carved word in the post to which an iron gate, long gone, was once attached. ASYLUM. A strange word, and a great-grandchild will likely mispronounce it at first, as I remember I did when I was learning to read.

"What's that? What was it for?"

I will write it down here, and this is what they will read, as an answer.

But where to begin?

I will begin with myself. Katy Thatcher. Here I am, thirteen, wearing a sailor dress in this old photograph, looking solemn (but proud, too; the dress was a new one, and I felt grown up). I *was*, I think, a solemn girl: Henry and Caroline Thatcher's oldest child, and for eight years their only.

Our house on Orchard Street was large, and to the side of the big shingled house, its entrance approached from a pebbled walk through the yard (the walk was between oak trees, and Levi, the stable boy who tended the horses and did odd jobs, spent many days in fall raking it bare), was my father's office. A small sign at the side gate read HENRY THATCHER, M.D. From my bedroom window above the porch roof, I could see patients unlatch the gate and make their way to that door, bringing their babies, their arthritis, their small aches and larger sufferings, to my father.

By thirteen I already knew that I wanted to be a doctor, too. I read accounts in the news of the war that was raging in Europe, and I could not wrap my mind around the reasons for it or the terrible logistics of battles far away. I listened to my parents talking to their friends, our next-door neighbors, Mr. and Mrs. Bishop, as they fretted over their oldest boy, Paul, who was just finishing Princeton then and should have been look-ing ahead to law school and to joining his father's firm one day. But Paul was already yearning to enlist in a war that had not yet, in 1915, begun to take American boys.

But at thirteen, when I read the war news, I thought only of the wounded and how if I were a doctor I could set their bones and heal their burns. I had watched my father do so many times.

I was not yet four when San Francisco toppled in an earthquake and burned. Even so young, I heard talk of it.

At eight, I had heard of the terrible fire in New York, of the factory girls, scores of them, leaping from the windows, their clothes aflame, and dying, burned and mangled, on the sidewalk while people watched in horror. My mother had said "Shhh" to Father when she saw me listening, but he, seeing that my interest was real and not just a child's curiosity, spoke to me of it later. Though I was still a child, we talked of the ways in which death comes, and how perhaps, not always, but sometimes, a doctor could push death away, could hold it back, or at the very least make it come easily.

By thirteen, by the time I had the sailor dress of which I was so proud, many of those moments were past. San Francisco had been rebuilt. The Triangle Shirtwaist Company fire had brought about new laws to protect factory workers.

And on the edge of town, when I was thirteen, stood the stone building called the Asylum. It still stands there today, though newspaper editorials call it the Eyesore in an attempt at wit, and there is talk of tearing it down to make room for a housing development. Its windows are boarded over now, and the grounds are littered with debris. Sometimes, in my growing-up years, when Austin was my beau, we would walk out that way, holding hands. Sometimes I found myself glancing at the ground, wondering if I would spot the gleam and flicker of a cat's-eye marble dropped by a boy. I wondered, then, as I still do, about the boy who had once given me a kitten and changed my life forever. His name was Jacob Stoltz.

His is the story I mean to write down now.

1. SEPTEMBER 1908

My friend Austin Bishop lived next door and was to be invited to my sixth birthday party the next month. Austin was already six and said that he could read. I thought it was true because he showed me a book with a story in it and told me the story—it was about a mouse—and then he told me the story again, and the words were exactly the same. Reading, I knew, was what made the words always, always be the same.

Jessie Wood was to come to my party, too, and had told me a secret, that she was bringing me a tea set with pink flowers as a birthday present.

She had promised her mother that she would not tell. A promise was a very important, very grown-up thing, and if I promised not to tell something, I would never ever tell. But Jessie was often naughty. She disobeyed. She told me that the pink flowers were roses and the tea set was real china.

Austin's brother, Paul, was not invited because he was too big. Paul was almost fifteen years old and had his own desk, many pencils, and a book with maps. He had a pocketknife that was very sharp and we were not to touch it, ever. He tried to smoke his father's pipe but he was too young, and it made him sick. We saw him being sick out by the barn. It was yellow and splattered on his shoes.

Austin's father was named Mr. Bishop, and he was a lawyer, but at home he spent a lot of time out in the barn, pounding and sawing. He liked tools and steam engines and wheels and anything that moved its parts and made noise. Sometimes he said he wished he could be a train engineer. During the summer, when Austin's birthday was coming, Mr. Bishop and Paul worked many days out in the barn. It was a secret. No one could peek. They made a lot of noise, and it was a surprise for Austin's birthday.

My mother said, when she saw what they had made, that it was a mazing. I had never seen a mazing before. It had wheels, but it was not a velocipede. *Everyone* had a velocipede, even me.

I was allowed to ride mine to the mailbox, but then I was always to turn around and come back.

Austin could sit in his mazing. He pushed with his feet on the pedals and he traveled down the walk. I supposed he could go to town in the mazing if he wished. Perhaps he could go to his father's office. Or to the library, or Whittaker's Dry Goods! A mazing could go anywhere.

I hoped that someone was building me a mazing for my birthday, but I didn't think that anyone was because there was no noise coming from the Bishops' barn or from our stable, except the plain old noise of the horses snorting and stamping their feet as Levi cleaned their stalls.

Our horses were named Jed and Dahlia, and they were brown but their manes and tails were black. Our cook was named Naomi, and she was also brown. Everything has a color, I remember thinking. I could not think of a single thing that had no color, except the water in my bath. You could see through water, I realized—could see your own hand when you tried to hold water in it, but then it ran away, right through your fingers, no matter how hard you tried to keep it there.

Austin had one more thing besides the mazing, one more thing that I wished I had. He had a baby sister! She had horrid black hair and cried a lot and her name was Laura Paisley Bishop.

How they got Laura Paisley was very, very

interesting to me. Austin's Nana took him on the train to Philadelphia for a whole day. How I wished my grandmother would do that for me! My own Gram lived in Cincinnati and came by train in the summers to visit, but she never took me with her on the train. Austin said it was noisy and clattery and you could look through the windows and see trees go by as fast as anything. Sometimes, when the train was going around a curve, you could look ahead and see the engine and know that you were part of it, still attached. It was hard to imagine.

They rode to Philadelphia and went to a museum, where they saw stuffed creatures, like bears, posing as if they were alive, and then they had lunch in a restaurant, with strawberry ice cream for dessert. Then they went back to the train station and came all the way home on the train again. When they arrived at our town, Austin's Nana used the telephone at the railroad station to call his home and see if anything exciting had happened while they were away.

"My goodness!" she said to Austin, then. "There will be quite a surprise at your house when we get there."

So they walked all the way home from the station, and when they got to Austin's house, he saw the surprise. It was a baby sister!

They had found her out in the garden. That's

what they told Austin: that his mother had gone outside to pick some tomatoes for lunch, and when she looked down, she saw a lovely baby girl there.

"Fibber!" I said to Austin.

I did not believe him because I had been playing in my own backyard almost all day, and never once heard a baby, and did not see Mrs. Bishop go out with her tomato basket at all. In fact, my mother had told me to play quietly because Mrs. Bishop had a headache and was lying down most of the day.

So I called Austin a fibber and he was angry and threw some dirt at me and said I could never hold his baby. But I asked my mother later and she said it was true that Mrs. Bishop had found the baby in the garden. Mother said that she hoped someday we would find one in ours.

So I decided I would look carefully each day. But it seemed a very strange thing, that babies appeared in gardens, because it might be raining. Or it might even be winter! I hoped that the babies were bundled up in thick blankets then!

I had to apologize to Austin for calling him a fibber. His big brother, Paul, was there when I did, and Paul laughed and said I shouldn't bother. Paul said I was the smartest child on the street. (It was not true, because I couldn't read yet, no matter how I tried.) But his mother, who was sitting in a rocking chair holding Laura Paisley, said,

"Shhhhh," so Paul shushed and went away and slammed the screen door behind him, which startled the baby, so that her eyes opened wide for a second and then closed again.

I hoped her hair would improve because it really was horrid to look at. It was exactly like Jed and Dahlia's manes.

2. SEPTEMBER 1910

Father took me with him to the country to get the new hired girl. It was a Sunday afternoon in late September; I had just started second grade, and I would very soon be eight. My teacher's name was Miss Dunbar, and I loved her desperately, but the stories that we read in the classroom, filled with children who were helpful and kind and had very nice clothes, didn't hold my interest. I wanted to know more about people who *needed* things. My mother, sympathetic with my impatience, had been reading books to me at home. I had loved listening to *Little Women* because of the missing father, the shortness of money, and the death of Beth, which I felt quite certain Father could have prevented if he had only been called in soon enough.

As we jiggled along, Father and I, in the crisp blue afternoon, behind the horses, I read the names on the mailboxes.

"Look for *Stoltz*," Father told me, and spelled it.

But after a while, he and I both laughed. There were too many named Stoltz. A prosperous farm with a huge red barn and low white fencing around the cornfields had STOLTZ on the mailbox; but so did another, closer to the road, that needed paint and a new roof.

"All cousins, I imagine," Father said. "The farm we want is up around the next bend, beyond that little grove of pine trees." He tapped the buggy whip gently on Jed's back so that the horses would continue along the dirt road. They slyly, lazily slowed their trot to a plod if we weren't paying attention.

I thought what it would be like to have cousins nearby. My own cousins lived in Cincinnati and I had never met them, only heard about them in letters that my mother read aloud. Maybe someday, Mother said, they could come to visit us by train.

But Peggy Stoltz, the girl we were coming to collect, had grown up here, where she could run through the pine grove and then—I pictured her, barefoot, in summer, with a dog scampering back and forth beside her—she could spend the afternoon playing with her cousins, probably wading in the stream that Father and I had just crossed, the horses' hooves thumping on the bridge. Maybe they went fishing, or caught butterflies. Maybe they went into the hen house and slipped their hands under the fat, steamy bellies of hens to find the warm, hidden eggs.

But when we rounded the bend and I saw Peggy Stoltz's home, I knew that her summers were not carefree ones. It was tidy but stark. It was poor.

It was why, at not quite fifteen years old, Peggy Stoltz was leaving school and becoming a hired girl. There was nothing for her here. My seven-year-old perception saw in an instant the contrast between our house and the one Peggy would be leaving.

The horses turned into the dooryard at Father's direction. Then they slowed, stopped, shook their heads, and snorted. "Mrs. Stoltz," Father said, and tipped his hat.

Peggy's mother had been standing in the yard, probably watching for our buggy. She smiled slightly and nodded. "Doctor Thatcher," she said in reply. Then she pointed with a smile to a toddler, made chubby with coat, standing wide-eyed beside her. "This is the one that caused us such worry. Look at her now."

Father secured the reins, set the buggy whip upright in its slot, and climbed down. He lifted me to the ground and then he leaned down toward the small girl, buttoned into a thick coat, who was frowning suspiciously at both him and me.

"Anna, is it? Do I remember it correctly?" Father asked Mrs. Stoltz, as he stood, and I saw the little one look up curiously at the sound of her own name.

"She had diphtheria last winter," Father told me. "I spent some long nights at this farm. But look at her rosy cheeks now!"

"She's very well, and into no end of mischief," Mrs. Stoltz said. "We have you to thank. Not for the mischief, though," she added, smiling.

"This is Katy," my father said. He nodded toward me. I held out my hand the way I'd been taught, and she shook it.

"Come inside. Our Peggy's just getting her things together. I can give you coffee, and milk for your girl."

But at that moment, Peggy Stoltz pushed open the screen door and appeared on the porch, holding a bag. "Thank you," Father said, "but we'll go on. It's four miles back, and if I let the horses rest they'll not want to start up again."

I knew it wasn't true. The horses were obedient and strong. But I could tell, also, that Father didn't want to go into the woman's house, to drink her coffee, to prolong her goodbye to her daughter. He didn't want to shame or sadden her. He took the bag from Peggy and hoisted it into the back of the buggy next to the medical bag that he always carried there.

"She's a hard worker," her mother said, "and a good girl." She picked up Anna, and the toddler wrapped her legs around her mother's hip as if to ride.

"We'll be good to your daughter, Mrs. Stoltz," Father said, "and my wife will be grateful for her help."

Peggy hadn't said anything at all. She simply stood, like someone accustomed to waiting. She had, I thought, a pretty face, with cheeks as pink as her little sister's; you could see a strength in it, too, and that one day she would look like her mother, proud and loving. Her brown hair was pulled up and back but the breeze pulled it away and it flew in wisps around her face.

Father lifted me to the buggy seat and as he did, Peggy went to her mother and hugged her, wrapping her arms around the little one, too, who began to wail. "Want my Peg," the little girl cried, holding out her arms, but by then Father was helping Peggy up into the seat beside me. Mrs. Stoltz said, "Be sure to give Nellie our love." Then she hushed the little girl and turned away. At a window of the house, I saw a curtain move aside, and a face appeared; then a hand, pressed against the glass. I thought Peggy ought to know. I nudged her and pointed to the window.

"That's Jacob," Peggy explained to me, the first words I heard her say. She waved to the face in the window, and after a moment the curtain dropped back and the boy disappeared behind it.

There was a Jacob in my school, a fourth-grader, and I wondered if it was the same boy. Farm children came into town for school, some of them, until they left to work the farms or, as Peggy, to hire out.

"How old is he? Does he go to school?" I asked, as the horses started up and Father clucked at them and turned them into the road. I felt shy with Peggy; she was new to me.

She shook her head. "Just turned thirteen," she said. "He don't go to school. He never could. He's touched."

Touched in the head, she meant. I had heard the phrase before, had never known exactly what it meant, but it didn't feel polite to ask anything more. As we moved at a trot down the road and the Stoltz house disappeared behind us, I thought of the boy's face through the window, and the way he had slowly raised his hand to say goodbye to his big sister.

I liked Peggy, liked feeling her beside me as we jiggled together in the buggy behind the horses eager for home and oats; she was solid and warm and she smelled good, like soap and garden earth. I saw her hands in her lap and could see that they were shaped and hardened by work. There was a new scratch, pink and ragged, across the back of her right hand, and I touched it, without thinking.

She smiled. "Kitten," she said. "It meant no harm."

Many of the families in our neighborhood had hired girls. They came in from the farms, leaving their large families behind with one less mouth to feed, usually in fall after helping with the harvest. They moved into attic rooms, doing the housework and laundry, helping mothers with new babies. They were accustomed to cold bedrooms and hard work. Indoor plumbing was new to many of the hired girls.

Some of them didn't stay long. They met town boys and married, or saved their money for secretarial school and went off to better themselves.

Peggy's sister Nell lived next door, in the Bishops' attic. I saw her every day in the yard, hanging up the laundry to dry. She helped Mrs. Bishop take care of Laura Paisley, who was lively and curious and into everything, now that she was two. When I went to play with Austin, Nell pushed the mop through our toys, pretending she was going to mop us up. She was strong and pretty, with a great halo of bright red hair, and Austin said she made them all laugh. But I heard Mrs. Bishop tell Mother that she was afraid Nell would leave them. She had just turned sixteen but she had ambitions, Mrs. Bishop said, as if *ambitions* meant measles, something we should try not to catch.

Peggy seemed quieter, more serious, and even her hair was a subdued brown, with none of the flamboyance of her sister's. Mother greeted her and showed her around the house; I followed behind, not wanting to be left out. I had already helped Mother tidy the little bedroom Peggy would have on the third floor, and I watched to see if she would appreciate the quilt I had chosen for her bed, a pink and white one that matched the colors in the flowered curtains. I could see that Peggy liked her room. Mother went downstairs, but I stayed and watched while she opened her bag and put her things away. She didn't have a lot. She hung two dresses in the old wardrobe and put a Bible and a hairbrush on the dresser.

"Look through the window," I told her. "See over there? The next house?"

She looked where I was pointing.

"That's the Bishops' house. And your sister's room is there, through the maple tree. When the leaves are gone you'll be able to see Nell's window."

"Really? I'll see Nellie's window?" Peggy smiled at the thought. "My sister and me, we had a room together at home, till she left."

"Did you miss her when she went?"

Peggy nodded. "But she was wild to go. She wanted desperately to be in town. She wanted to go to the pictures."

"The pictures!" I started to giggle. "Have you ever been?"

Peggy said no. "But Nell did. A fellow took her once. She saw Mary Pickford. She tried to fix her hair like that. She rolled it up in rags and it made curls, but they didn't last. My mother said she was foolish."

I thought of Nell's hair, thick and flame-bright, always pinned back as she did the housework but somehow untidy still.

"She uses rouge sometimes," Peggy confided. "And she plans to change her name to Evangeline Emerson. You need a fancy name for moving pictures. She wants to be in pictures someday."

"Do you?"

"Oh my, no! I never! I'll save my money and help my parents, and someday I'll find a nice steady fellow and get married."

"Maybe someday we'll go to the pictures and see Nellie," I told her. "She'll be famous! She'll have lots of beaus."

Peggy smiled. She peered into the looking glass over the dresser and smoothed her hair. I noticed the scratch on her hand again.

"Will you miss your kitten?" I asked her. "Even if it scratched?"

She smiled and said no. "We have a barn full of kittens," she said. "There are always new ones."

"Oh, I wish I could have one. Mother says a dog is enough. Did you meet our dog when you came in? He won't come up here because he's very old and his hips hurt."

"He greeted me at the door, remember?" Peggy said. "What was his name?"

"Pepper. My favorite book right now is called *The Five Little Peppers and How They Grew*. It's about a family whose father is dead, and they live in a little brown house and it is so hard for them to pay the rent; they are *always* worried. And guess what they eat for breakfast!"

Peggy, arranging things in a drawer, thought for moment. "Oatmeal," she suggested.

"No, you'll never guess. *Cold potatoes.* Isn't it awful? But it's all they have, poor things. They are so needy! But always cheerful. Mother is reading me a chapter each night. Do you have a favorite book?"

Peggy glanced at the Bible on the table but then shook her head. "I've never had books," she said.

"Now you will! We have a whole bookcase full, and you can read whatever you want! We can go to the library, too."

"What's in there?" Peggy asked, and she pointed to the door across the hall from her bedroom as we started down the stairs.

"The attic! Want to see? It's scary. There are mice."

Peggy laughed. "Mice are nothing to be scared of. But maybe you *do* need a cat."

I opened the door to the unfinished part of the third floor and let Peggy peek in. There were windows, so it wasn't dark. But it was rough, with cobwebbed beams across the top, and dust every-where. We could see the shape of trunks, and stacked boxes.

"My own baby clothes are in that trunk there in the corner," I told Peggy, and pointed. "Mother let me have a few things for my doll, but we're saving all the nice clothes because maybe someday we will have another baby."

Peggy smiled.

"And see there? The trunk with the curved top? My grandmother's wedding gown is in there, and if I want, I can wear it when I get married. But I mustn't grow too much, because my grandmother was very small. I'll show you sometime."

"I must go down now," Peggy said. "Your mother will be wondering where I am."

So I closed the attic door and followed her down to the kitchen, where Pepper was sleeping in the corner. Naomi left work early on Sundays—she never missed the Sunday evening service at her church—but she had made us an apple pie, and Mother had put it into the oven to warm. The whole house was fragrant. I watched as Peggy put on the apron Mother gave her. I could tell from the look of her—her flushed cheeks, her slow smile, and the way she tied the apron with her strong hands—that she liked us, liked our house, and that she would be happy here.

But I wondered about Jacob, the touched boy, and how he felt to have his second big sister taken away.

3. OCTOBER 1910

Jacob Stoltz was standing beside the road when Father took me with him to the country one Saturday morning in October, just after my eighth birthday. I was recovering from chicken pox, and Father said the fresh air would perk me up. I was startled to see Peggy's brother there, because we were not very near the Stoltz farm. We were going toward the flour mill, out the Lawton County Road. One of the helpers at the mill had cut his hand badly, on a piece of machinery. Father had stitched it, he told me, just the way the seamstress, Miss Abbott, might stitch fabric together with her shiny needle tapping against the thimble on her other hand.

"Not like the hem of your dress, Katydid," Father said, as I turned over the edge on my knees to look at Miss Abbott's neat stitches, which barely showed. "More like the way she sews satin binding on the edge of a blanket, bigger stitches. And I use special very strong thread. Today I'll pull the stitches out if the wound has healed."

As it happened, there was a worn blanket folded in the back of the buggy, under Father's bag. I turned around and tugged at it so that I could examine the stitches and imagine how they would look in the flesh of a hand.

That was when I felt Father pull back on the reins so that the buggy slowed to a stop. "It's Peggy's brother," he said. "Shall we give him a ride?"

I dropped the corner of the blanket I'd been examining and turned to look down at the boy who had appeared suddenly at the roadside. I had seen him only once before: the blurred face in the window the day we had picked up Peggy from the farm a month before. I remembered that he was thirteen, five years older than I. He was thin, I saw now, and tall for his age, and, I thought, still growing fast, for his overalls were riding up his ankles and he would soon need longer. He was wearing a cap that brimmed his forehead, and he looked up at us from its shadow.

"Hello there, Jacob," I heard Father say. "Did you sense we'd be along this way? You certainly wander about. You're a far piece from home."

The boy's look was not one of recognition, though Father knew him and called him by name, but it was not fearful or suspicious, either.

"This is my daughter, Katy. We're going to Schuyler's Mill," Father told him, as if they were to have a normal conversation. "But we won't be there long, and we could take you home after, if you'd like to ride with us."

The boy turned and looked at the horses. His face changed and softened.

Father reached into the basket that Mother had placed by my feet. He took out two apples and handed them down. "Here, Jacob," Father said. "Give them a treat. Then hop up on the back."

"They're Jed and Dahlia," I told him. "Dahlia's the one with the white by her nose."

The boy's expression didn't change. He held the apples one by one to the big wrinkled mouths and waited while the horses chewed, shaking their heads and dripping juice onto the road. Then he went to the buggy behind me and hauled himself up.

He made a clucking noise, imitating Father's voice to the horses as we started up. I could see Father smile at the sound. "You like those horses, don't you, Jacob?" he said. "And the mill, too.

26

Remember? You went with me before. You liked the gears and wheels, how they turned."

"When did you take him?" I asked, pulling at my father's sleeve a little. He had taken me to the mill before. But it surprised me, if he had taken this strange boy, and made me a little jealous, to think of someone else sitting beside Father in the buggy, in my place.

Father chuckled and gathered me against his side in a kind of hug. "You're in school most days now, Katy, and sometimes I like the company of a quiet boy like this one. Isn't that right, Jacob?"

I turned my head and looked back at him, but he ducked down so I couldn't see his face under the cap that he wore. Then, as I watched, he moved his hands against his own knees and made a sound— *shoooda, shoooda, shoooda*—and I recognized it as the sound of the great grindstone moving over the grain, crushing it; and with the sound, Jacob's hands were making the slow circles in the same rhythm.

"*Shoooda, shoooda, shoooda,*" I said with him, hoping, I suppose, to make a game of it, but he took no notice.

Schuyler's Creek, slow-moving and shallow, was the same stream that ran near the Stoltz farm and was where Peggy and her sister, she had told me, used to drop their shoes and stockings on the bank and wade, holding their skirts and aprons up to keep them dry. But someplace in the miles between the Stoltz farmland and the mill, the creek changed. Father said the land went downhill and so the creek had to fall, dropping down over rocks as it carved its way, and growing faster as it fell.

I had seen pictures of the big waterfall at Niagara. Mother and Father took their wedding trip to Niagara Falls and had told me of it, the water as high as a mountain, roaring downward, sending spray into the air and collecting rainbows as it did. There was a postcard in our album at home, hand-colored, with Mother's neat penmanship beneath, explaining that it was Niagara Falls, New York, 1898.

Our little stream, Schuyler's Creek, was nothing like that. But it did rush downhill, and by the time it reached Schuyler's Mill, it was a furious thing, bubbling and racing into the great wooden wheel that took it up and turned it somehow into power.

The mill itself was a huge stone building three stories high, larger than our Presbyterian church, but with no bells. It had its own noises: the rushing noise of the water, the creaking of the wheel, and the heavy turning of the parts my father said were called the gears. Inside, there was the *shoooda, shoooda, shoooda* of the great grind-stone. But there were also the sounds of men's shouts as they filled the wagons, the crunch of gravel under the wagon wheels, the clop of hooves—mules and horses—and the snapping of whips as the creatures strained to pull the heavy loads away.

The men and mules and horses all paused when we arrived, and the men tipped their hats to my father. "Doctor," some said. "Doctor Thatcher," said others. I sat straight beside him, proud. And I could feel Jacob stop his chanting sounds in the back of the buggy and sit straight, too.

Someone took the horses' reins and held them still. Another man reached into the back and took my father's bag. I waited, biting my lip and hoping Father would not make me wait in the buggy. But he reached for me after he was on the ground, and swung me down and held my hand.

"The boy can carry my bag," he said. The man handed it to Jacob.

I heard one man say something to another. "Imbecile," he said; he nudged the man beside him and pointed to Jacob. I wasn't certain what the word meant, but I could see that it was not meant kindly and hoped that Jacob hadn't heard.

We went with Father up the steps and entered the mill. It was dark, warm, and noisy, with each different sound playing its part, like the band concerts I had heard in summer in the town park. Austin and Jessie and I would run about the park on those summer evenings, chasing fireflies and watching the young women in their pretty dresses flirt with the boys. In the background was the music, with bright brass instruments leading the way, but up close, as we played near the bandstand and listened, we could hear the little ones—the flutes and even sometimes a tiny triangle held in the air for a moment to be touched—each putting in its sound.

Here in the mill, it was the great whooshing sound of the wheel and the splash and thunder of water, over everything. The crackle and swish of poured grain. Then the creak and grind of the wooden gears, and the deep smooth sound of the stone. Finally there were the small, almost silent sounds of the finished flour dropping into bags, and the soft thud of the bags being stacked.

I was sorry when Father led us into the office and closed the door against the sound. But I sat where he directed me and was still. Jacob set the bag down where Father pointed and in a minute the man with the bandaged hand came in, holding his hat in front of him, and nodded. "Doctor," he said, as the others had.

I didn't notice Jacob slip away. When Father opened his bag, my mind went there, as it always did, to his shiny tools and the bottles with their special smells. He had once given me a little bag so that I could doctor my dolls, and it was filled with small things, imitations, not real, and though I played with it because I knew he wished me to, I had no affection for the sugar pills or the dull scissors. I loved only the smells and the sharpness and the real importance of the tools my father used for healing.

I watched carefully as he unwrapped the man's thickly bandaged hand. "Good," he said. "You've kept it clean. There's no infection.

"Look, Katy," he told me, and nodded when I left my chair and came close, though the man with the wound seemed surprised.

The stitching thread was black against the man's pale skin. His other hand was ruddy and dark, like all workingmen's hands, but the bandage had kept the light and labor from the wounded one and made it pale. I could see where the jagged cut, shaped like a drawing of a lightning bolt, zigzagged across his palm, ending in the soft flesh at the base of his thumb.

"Move your fingers, Sturges," my father said, and when the man did, he nodded.

"Good. Now the thumb." While I watched, the large thumb bent and straightened. "Any pain?"

"Stiff is all," the man said.

"And you can feel? Try this against your fingertips. Do you make it out as chain and not a piece of wood or maybe rope?" Father handed him his watch chain and the man rolled it back and forth, and nodded. "Gold chain," he said, and grinned.

"You're a lucky man, Sturges. No real damage. Now you won't mind if I show my daughter? She wants to be a doctor."

I moved closer and Father showed me, running his own thumb across the pattern of dark stitches.

"It was the palmar fascia that protected him from worse injury," Father said. "It's very thick and strong tissue here. Below it are the nerves and muscles, and if he had sliced into those, we'd have had to haul him into town and do some pretty complicated surgery."

"Wouldn't have gone," the man muttered.

"You'd've gone or lost your hand, Sturges," Father said, laughing. He began rubbing the area of the stitches with gauze soaked from a bottle in his bag. The smell was strong and medicinal, but the liquid had no color and it dried quickly. Then Father lifted one of the stitches with a pincer in one hand, snipped it with sharp scissors in his other, pulled it through, and laid the snipped thread on a piece of gauze set out on the desk. It didn't seem to hurt the man at all. I counted as Father did it again and again.

"Sixteen," I announced, when he was done.

With the black stitches gone, I could see only a jagged pink line on the man's palm, and some tiny dots where the stitches had been. It seemed astonishing to me, to have what had seemed a terrible wound be gone entirely, turned to a faint pink line.

The man named Sturges seemed surprised as well, and kept opening and closing his hand as if he had newly learned to do it.

"Keep it clean, still," Father told him. "Wear a glove on it when you're working. And keep it limber. Sometimes a scar like that will tighten. You don't want that." He wrapped the tools he had used in a strip of cloth and replaced them in the bag. I knew why he wrapped them, because he had told me once. You could never use an instrument twice, because it might carry infection. So you wrap them and keep them set aside after they are used, until they could be properly cleaned. I tried to do it with my little toy bag of instruments, but it didn't seem to matter, really, and some of them couldn't hold together for being washed, anyway.

They shook hands, and I saw the man open and close his injured one again, after shaking, as if he were still surprised that it worked. Then he nodded to me, and said "Miss" before he turned and left.

Father snapped his bag closed, looked around, and sighed. "That boy," he said. "He slipped off while we were busy. He did it last time, too."

I was frightened. The mill with its noisy parts seemed dangerous, now that Jacob had disappeared into it. But Father told me not to worry. "I know where to find him," he said, and took my hand. "You hold on to me now, though, Katy. Here, Jackson, put this in my buggy, would you?" He handed his medical bag to the clerk who sat at a table outside the office door.

With Father's hand tight around mine, I followed him into the huge open section of the mill, where flecks of grain spun against the daylight that came in from narrow windows. Off to one side I saw workers who were dusted with flour so that their faces looked ghostly. One man laughed, and his open mouth was dark against the powdered face. I knew he was only a man, but I held Father's hand tighter while we looked for Jacob.

"He'll be by the grindstone," Father said, leaning down so that I could hear him against the noise of gears and workers. "He likes that big stone. You heard him in the buggy, making the sound."

"Father?" I asked. "Is he an imbecile? Is that what it is, to be touched in the head?"

"I wouldn't call Jacob that," Father said firmly, "because *imbecile* means having no brains. And Jacob, he's *different,* all right, but he knows how to go to what he loves, and how to stay safe near it. That takes brains, I'd say. Katy—there he is."

I looked over and saw Jacob in the shadows, watching the great stone turn and grind. He was rocking back and forth where he stood, and though I couldn't hear, I saw his hands moving at his sides and knew that he must be murmuring, *"Shoooda, shoooda, shoooda."* Father was right that he knew to stay safe, out of the way, and I saw that the sound and rhythm of the turning grindstone made him happy.

When Father told him it was time to go, he pretended he didn't hear. He had a funny way of doing it. He put his hands up to cover his ears, and he continued his rocking and humming. But Father touched him firmly again and mentioned the horses. "We'll give the horses a bit of grain before we leave," he told Jacob. And so he came.

We left the mill to find that the back of the buggy was piled with sacks of flour as payment. Jacob fed each horse a handful of grain and then climbed up and sat atop the flour sacks, his cap pulled low over his forehead.

We took the long way home, past the Stoltz farm, and left Peggy's brother there with a bag of flour for his family. Before he took it, he touched the necks of the horses and made a sound to them, though he said no human goodbye to us. A dog dashed to the buggy to greet him; and I saw, as he turned and walked to his own barn, carrying the flour, that two cats ran out from the shadows there, rubbed against him, matched their steps to his, and followed him in.

4. NOVEMBER 1910

Mother wasn't feeling well and so most mornings Peggy helped me get ready for school.

"If Jacob can't go to school," I asked her one morning as she brushed my hair, "then why can he roam all around the way he does? If I have the sniffles and can't go to school, Mother makes me stay in bed all day and drink hot water with lemon and sugar in it. And I had to stay in the house *forever* when I had chicken pox. But not Jacob. Father says he sees him often, very far from home. And I think he has even been here, behind our house. Levi saw him. That's four miles!"

"Jacob's been here? Are you certain? Hand me that ribbon," Peggy said, and I gave her the brown ribbon that matched the plaid of my school dress.

"Ow, don't pull so tight."

Peggy was good at braiding my hair, but sometimes she went too hard at it, trying to make it neat.

"The stable boy, Levi. He told Father."

"He told your father what? Now hold still, don't wiggle."

"He told Father that a boy comes sometimes and slips in and stands by the horses. He strokes their noses, the boy does. Levi called him a deaf-mute. But Father said no. Father said it must be Jacob, because Jacob loves the horses, but that Jacob is not a deaf-mute at all. He can hear. And Father says that though he doesn't talk like you and me, there is meaning to the sounds he makes."

Peggy nodded. "That's true."

"Why do I have to go to school, but Jacob doesn't? I would like to roam around all day in the country. I would climb trees and feed cows and and—" I thought, but nothing else came to my mind. I really didn't know what country children did. "I would play all day, the way Jacob does," I said, finally.

Peggy finished tying the ribbon at the end of the braid she had made in my hair. She straightened the sides of the bow. "There. Done," she said.

"And I would never wear a hair ribbon, either."

"You look pretty. Most girls like to look pretty." Peggy was laughing as she put the brush away and began to smooth my bedcovers.

"Anyway," she added, "Jacob don't have the sniffles or chicken pox. He's just different from most, and can't learn from books. But he don't play all day. Yes, he roams a bit. But he gets his chores done. He helps with the animals. Jacob's better than anyone with animals. It don't surprise me that he visits your horses."

"Does he comb and brush your horses at home? Levi brushes ours." I had been thinking that I might try to talk the stable boy into letting me braid Jed and Dahlia's manes, the way Peggy had just done mine.

"I suppose. And feeds them. And he watches out for the calves and lambs when they come. Sometimes they need extra care."

"Kittens, too," I said. "They probably need care."

"Come on, Naomi has your breakfast ready. Be quiet going past your mama's door. She's sleeping." Peggy started for the stairs and I followed her, tiptoeing past my parents' bedroom.

"I wish I had a kitten."

"Well, our barn is full of them. That old tomcat chases the females around the barn and every time we turn around, it seems there's a new batch of kittens."

"What's a tomcat?"

Peggy chuckled. "He's a big old fella all full of himself who takes advantage of the females and next thing they know, they have kittens. Think old Tomcat stays around to help out? Not a chance. He's off looking for a new lady friend by then."

I chuckled too, not because I understood, but because Peggy made a funny gesture with her arms, imitating a stealthy cat on the prowl. "I do love kittens, though," I told her.

"Sometimes when a new litter comes and there are just too many, Jacob has to drown them."

I stopped at the foot of the stairs. "Drown?" I asked.

Peggy looked back at me. "It's what they do on farms, Katy. It's the kindest thing when there are too many. They don't know. It don't hurt them any. Jacob takes them down to the creek and it only takes a minute."

I stared at her in horror. *Kittens?*

"He's a gentle boy, Jacob is," she explained. "He wouldn't hurt nothing, ever."

I pondered for a moment, deciding how to feel about this. "Like when I step on ants, I suppose," I said at last. "They don't even know. Do you think it's the same, Peggy?"

"I guess. We don't need to think about it. Look! Naomi made pancakes!"

But I did think about it. I thought about the

touched boy, his soft look the day that he had held apples to our horses' mouths, and his gentle hands making the rhythm of the great grindstone against his thin, denim-covered thighs. I thought about his holding newborn kittens, so tiny, touching their fur with his fingers, and then lowering them into the creek and holding them under. The kindest thing, Peggy had said.

One morning late in November I found the Sears Roebuck catalogue open on Mother's desk in the parlor. I hoped she was planning to have a new dress made for me. Jessie Wood had a new one of black-and-white checks, with a sailor collar and red trim on the cuffs. She wore it to school, and I was jealous.

Usually Mother just looked at the pictures in the catalogue. Then she would have Miss Abbott, the seamstress, come. Miss Abbott would measure me all over while I stood on a stool. Mother would show her a picture and give her the fabric she had bought at Whittaker's store. Miss Abbott would study the picture and cut out a paper pattern, holding it up to me to be sure it was the right size. Then she would go away, to her own small house down on Vine Street, near the dairy, and when she came back, she would have the dress partly made, all basted together.

This was the part I liked. I would put on the basted dress, very carefully so the stitches wouldn't break, and Mother would stand me on the kitchen table. Then Miss Abbott would carefully mark the hem with her little tool that puffed chalk in a line when she squeezed the bulb. I liked how the white line appeared all the way around the bottom of my dress. Then she would take it away again and do the final stitching, and soon it would look just like the dress in the picture Mother had chosen.

When I found the catalogue there, I turned the pages until I found one that showed little girls, and in my mind I chose the dress I wanted, though I knew Mother would say no. It was too fancy. Carefully I sounded out the words that described it: "White lawn trimmed with lace," it said below the picture. "Neat belt of silk ribbon with rosette in front." I didn't know the word *rosette,* but I could tell from the picture that it was a wonderful bunched thing like a flower, maybe a peony not quite in bloom.

"Look!" I told Peggy, when she came into the parlor with a dust cloth. I pointed to the picture. "Do you think Mother would ask Miss Abbott to make me this? It has a rosette. I know it's too elegant for school, but I certainly could wear it to birthday parties.

"If I ever have a birthday party," I added,

grumbling. My eighth birthday party the month before had been canceled because of my chicken pox.

Peggy studied the picture and smiled.

"Jessie's birthday is next month," I told her. "I'm older than she is, but she was a Christmas baby, which is nice, don't you think? I could wear it to Jessie's birthday party."

"It's pretty," Peggy agreed, "but you'd better turn the pages back to where your mother had it open. She's going to have some clothes made for herself."

"For herself? She doesn't need new clothes! I do! I've grown three inches this year!" Grumpily I flipped the pages away from the little girls in their lace-trimmed party dresses. "I don't remember which page it was on," I told Peggy.

"She'll be needing new clothes soon," Peggy said, and took the catalogue from me. "Here. This is the page." She laid it open again on Mother's desk.

"*Those* aren't very pretty." I peered at the drawing of ladies posing in their ordinary dresses. "What's this word, Peggy? I can't read it." I pointed with my finger to a word I'd never seen before and that didn't sound itself out easily.

Peggy looked. " 'Stylish,' " she read. "It's a hard word for a second-grader, even a good reader like you. Can you read the rest?"

"'And,'" I read. "That's an easy word." I faltered on the next one.

Peggy helped me. "'Practical.' That means 'useful.'"

"'Stylish and practical,'" I read. "Wait. Don't help me with the next one. It's long, but I can do it." I made the sounds under my breath and put them together. "'Maternity,'" I said. "Is that right?"

"Yes. You *are* a good reader."

"'Dresses,'" I finished. "Now listen. I'll read it all. 'Stylish and practical maternity dresses.'" I looked again at the catalogue page, where six women were standing in poses with their hands on their hips and their feet in pointed shoes, arranged as if they might begin to dance. Their smiles were forced and foolish, I thought, not at all like real smiles.

"What does *maternity* mean?" I asked Peggy. She had moved across the room and was pulling at the heavy draperies, rearranging their folds and shaking out dust. I could see the dust specks float slowly in the light from the window.

"Motherhood," Peggy said. She retied the heavy gold cord that held the draperies back. "Those women in the picture are going to be mothers."

"How do they know that?" I asked, looking again at the stupid smiling women in their stylish and practical maternity dresses. "Isn't it always a surprise when you find a baby? Austin's mother said she just happened to find Laura Paisley in the garden."

"Oh!" Peggy said, as if she were surprised. "Oh, I didn't mean—" She came over quickly and took the catalogue from me. "Look. I wanted to show you the pages where they show books. See here?" She sat down beside me on the sofa and pointed to the lists of books in the catalogue. "Here's one called *Card Tricks*! Imagine that! There wouldn't be a book about card tricks in the library, do you think?"

I laughed, thinking about the librarian, Miss Winslow, at the public library on Main Street. Peggy had a library card now, and she took me with her sometimes, on Thursday afternoons. Miss Winslow would disapprove of card tricks, I knew. But I thought Father would like the book. I wondered if we could get it for him for Christmas and decided to ask Mother.

And maybe, I thought, I would ask Mother, too, about the ladies in their motherhood dresses and how they knew that such a surprise would come their way.

But it was Father who explained. Mother was so flustered when I asked that she almost dropped her knitting.

"Well, my goodness!" she said. We were in the parlor after supper, and it was almost time for me to go to bed. "Did you hear that, Henry? Did you hear what Katy asked?"

He hadn't, because he was reading the newspaper, but when I repeated the question, he smiled. Not a flustered, nervous smile like Mother's, but his usual quiet smile, the one that moved his mustache into a curve. "You just come along with me, Katydid," he said, getting up from his chair. He folded the paper and put it on the table. "We'll go into my office and I will show you something wonderful."

"Henry, do you think—" Mother began. But I had already taken his hand.

"Well, put her coat on her, dear," she said. "It's cold out."

But it wasn't very cold, just nippy, as Naomi always said, and Father didn't bother with my coat. We had to go out the front door and across the yard, then into the side entrance that was just to his office, though it was still attached to our house.

Our house was never locked, but Father's office always was. He opened the office door with his big key, turned on the lights, and led me in. I loved Father's office. There was his large, important desk, and two chairs where sick people—they were called patients, I knew—could sit. And there was a long, narrow table where they could lie down, if he had to poke at their stomachs. One time, two summers before, he poked Paul Bishop's stomach and then sent him to the hospital and took his whole appendix out. Austin and I wanted ours taken out, too, so Father sat us both on the table together and poked at our stomachs so much that it tickled. Then he said we were fine, and he gave us each a taffy to eat.

There were cabinets where Father kept medicines and tools. Sometimes he gave me wooden tongue depressers to play with. I drew faces at one end and wrapped the other part with clothes scraps to make a dress. They weren't as real-looking as my doll with the bisque head, the one I called Princess Victoria, but Jessie and I could make a lot of them and then we held balls and cotillions and danced them around together.

I climbed up in one of the patients' chairs and watched while Father opened a cupboard and took out something like a statue. It was the stomach part of a lady. He set it on his desk, and then carefully he opened it up! It came apart just down the middle, and there inside you could see an upside-down baby with its eyes tightly closed and its little hands curled up. It *was* wonderful, just as he had said; and when he began to explain it to me, how the baby grew there, I could see that it all made sense; it was exactly right, much more right than finding it in the dirt with the cutworms and slugs under the tomatoes and summer squash.

"Me?" I asked him. "I grew like that?"

He said yes.

"And Austin? And Laura Paisley?"

He said yes.

"And Peggy? And Jessie? Jacob Stoltz? And—"

But he could tell that it was like when I tried to think of more people to bless, so that I wouldn't have to go to sleep. "God bless the postman," I would say, "and my cousins in Cincinnati—"

He closed the woman back up and hid her baby away. But I liked knowing it was there, and knowing now too that there was one like it inside my mother. "When?" I asked him. "What kind? And how long?"

He said spring. It took a long time. And we wouldn't know until it was born whether it would be a sister or a brother.

Then we turned out the lights and he took me home again, through our own yard and up our front steps, past the porch swing, and in through our own front door to where Mother was still sitting in the sitting room with her knitting in her hands, the white yarn going up and around, up and around. I could hear Peggy finishing the dishes in the kitchen. Naomi had hung up her apron, put on her jacket, and gone home, carrying a basket of leftovers for her own family.

"May I tell Peggy?" I asked.

Mother smiled. "She knows."

I ran to the kitchen anyway, to tell Peggy that now I knew, too.

It *was* Jacob in the stable. I knew it when the stable boy told Father. But I knew it for certain when I saw him there myself.

It was early evening, and I had been playing skip-rope on the front walk with Jessie until her mother called her home for supper. It was chilly out, Thanksgiving-soon weather, and there were still dead leaves in the yard, the last fallen not yet raked up. I thought to go in by the back door instead of the front so as to walk through the leaves, because I liked the feel of them on my feet and the sound of the whispery rustle they made.

When I neared the stable I saw a dog by the door, one I did not know, not one of the neighborhood pets. This one was brown with a white face, and it sat patiently the way dogs do when they are waiting. From inside I heard sounds: not just the stamp and snort and shiver of the horses, but the sounds of a boy's voice, a kind of singing.

Levi was already gone. After he fed and watered the horses each evening he always left to do his other odd jobs around town before going back to the little ramshackle house down near the railway station where he lived with his widowed mother and a great many younger brothers and sisters. A downright shame, Naomi said, that Levi's father had died two years ago of pneumonia, leaving that poor woman with all those little ones to raise alone and no chance, now, of any of them being educated.

It was not dark yet outside but I could see through the kitchen window that our lights were on, and I could see the figures of Naomi and Peggy moving by the stove and sink.

The stable door was partway open, and I pushed it further. Surely Jacob must have known I had entered because of the creak of the door and the whoosh of nippy outdoor air that blew in with me. But he didn't look over. He was stroking Jed's big, soft face, humming. From her stall, Dahlia watched; then she tossed her head and turned her dark eyes on me in a kind of question. So I went to her.

I wasn't afraid at all. Being with Jacob the day we took him to the mill, my father and I, had made me familiar with his gentleness, and Peggy, too, had spoken of his special way with animals, so I knew he was nothing to be wary of.

And I liked the sound he was making, a kind of singing that wasn't real singing at all. I wondered if he would mind my joining in, so I watched his face, tried to catch onto the same note, and kept at it when I saw that it didn't make him uneasy.

The horses seemed soothed by it. They stood quietly, and I stroked Dahlia as the touched boy was stroking Jed, so that we made a kind of rhythm with our hands and our humming.

I knew I would hear Mother call very soon and that I would have to go. So I went over to the oat barrel and took two handfuls. I knew I shouldn't, for horses must not have too many oats or they sicken. But the handfuls were small. I gave one to Jacob, pouring them into his open hand, and then we each gave our oats to a horse, the two huge wrinkled mouths opening and the long pink tongues coming out, eager and pleased.

"No more, though," I whispered to Jacob. "They mustn't have too much or they'll come down with colic."

Then I felt embarrassed to have said it. "You know that already," I told him. "Peggy says you tend the animals on the farm. It was foolish of me to remind you. I'm sorry."

But he paid no attention. He was back to stroking the great quivery nose of the horse.

"Katy! Supper!" My mother's voice came from the porch.

"I must go," I told Jacob politely.

"Remember, their names are Jed and Dahlia?" I said. "Jed's that one there."

"I'm Katy," I added. "Remember?"

He didn't look at me.

"Peggy's in our kitchen helping with supper," I said. "And your other sister, Nellie? She's next door. Right over there." I pointed toward the Bishops' house, through the open stable door.

"Katy!" My mother's voice again.

"Goodbye," I said hastily. I left him there and left the stable, calling to Mother as I ran toward the house. "Coming!"

From my bedroom window that night I looked down and saw that the door to the stable was closed and the brown dog had disappeared. I knew that the touched boy was gone, that he had run the four miles home through the dark. That night was the first frost. In the morning the last apples hung frozen in our tree.

5. DECEMBER 1910

Snow! When I woke, I could feel the silence of it. There was frost on my window, and the room was cold. It had been cold when I went to bed, but now it was a different kind of cold, a quiet kind.

I didn't get up at first. I snuggled there under my blue and white quilt, thinking about how it would look outside. The world changes so, with the first snow. Ghost shapes appear where bushes have been.

Finally I heard Father and Mother talking in their bedroom, and then I heard Father's footsteps on the stairs, and I knew he would tend the furnace, shoveling in some more coal, and the house would warm a bit. Doors opened and closed below. After a moment I heard Naomi arrive and stamp snow from her feet in the kitchen, and I pictured her starting the oatmeal.

The door to my room opened and Mother, wearing her blue dressing gown, looked in at me. She was over what Peggy had told me was called "morning sickness."

"No school today, Katy! Naomi barely made it here. If she had a telephone I would have called and told her not to come. Peggy and I could have made breakfast. But Naomi's a real soldier. She trudged right through it."

Mother's long hair was still down. I loved seeing mother with her hair that way; she looked like a young girl. I wondered if she remembered being eight. I wondered if she remembered the excitement of the first snow.

The Stevensons' tea towels were still on their porch clothesline, and Mother said that Mrs. Stevenson had probably scolded their hired girl for forgetting to bring them in last night.

"They'll be frozen solid," Peggy said. "She'll have to crack them in half and then dry them in the cellar."

I poured cream on my steaming oatmeal and

laughed at the thought of the Stevensons' hired girl breaking the icy tea towels. We had to do it, too, from time to time.

Father looked at his watch. He was in a hurry because he had patients to see, at the hospital. The ones with appointments at his office weren't urgent, and most of them wouldn't be able to get through the snow, anyway. But the youngest Cooper boy had mastoid surgery just yesterday—he had had a cholesteatoma in his right ear, Father said—and must be watched carefully for a while, or he would be deaf.

"And Mattie Washington," he added. "You must know her, Naomi. Her house is close to yours."

Naomi, still at the stove, nodded. "She doesn't have pain, does she?"

"No," Father told her. "But I want to be sure she's being kept comfortable. She'll go soon."

"Ninety-two," Naomi said. "Seven children, only three still left, and one of them was always worthless."

Father smiled. "Even the worthless one is at her side. And lots of grandchildren."

"And some greats," Naomi told him. "I believe she has some greats."

"Yes. She's lived a good long life." Father pulled his heavy coat on. We could hear the horses in front; Levi had brought them around. They stamped their feet, and the bells on their harnesses jingled. Horses like snow. It makes them excited, and I think they like the way their snorts make steam in the cold air. When Father opened the front door, I could hear one of them whinny. The light sliced into the hall when the door opened. The entire day was white, and I could see the flakes still drifting.

"The steps will be slippery, Henry. Be careful," Mother warned him, and then he was gone.

The steps *were* slippery, I found, when finally, bundled up, mittened, and booted, with a red knitted scarf wrapped twice around my neck and up over my chin, I went outside. Next door, Austin was already out, building a snowman in his front yard for his sister, Laura Paisley, who even at two and a half had learned how to command her brother.

"Make him a nose!" Laura Paisley called from the front porch, where she watched Austin at work. Her own nose and cheeks were pink with cold. She was wearing blue mittens.

"I will," Austin promised. "First I have to finish him." He was still patting the sides smooth, and I went over to help. It was hard, walking through the snow, which was up partway to my knees. On the way, I broke off two thin branches from the forsythias to use as snowman arms.

"Ding-dong!" Laura Paisley shouted suddenly, clapping her mittened hands in delight.

Bells! Not like the small jingles from our two horses harnessed to the buggy. But many bells, rows of them, because the snow-roller had come around the corner and entered our street, with its six huge horses. Slowly, dragging the heavy roller, they flattened the snow in the street. When Father left, Orchard Street was like a meadow, or a sea of snow, not a street at all. Jed and Dahlia had pranced through, lifting their feet high, leaving prints of their spiked winter shoes in the deep new snow. But now Orchard Street was reappearing. And in front of each house, now, men and boys were out with shovels, clearing the walks.

The Stevensons' hired girl came out onto their porch and took the frozen tea towels down. I thought she had been scolded. Her face was glum. But then she looked over, saw our snowman, and smiled. "Need a carrot?" she called. "I'll bring one out in a bit. And some lumps of coal for eyes."

Like our Peggy and Peggy's sister Nell, she was just a young girl, in from the farm, sending the money back home, to help out.

They were all slightly younger than Austin's brother, Paul Bishop, who would graduate next year from high school. Watching her unpin the towels, I wondered if she ever wished she could have stayed in school, studying French and algebra, instead of washing tea towels and scrubbing the kitchen floor for the Stevensons.

Nellie came out to check on Laura Paisley, and behind her came Paul, who was home because the high school had also closed for the day. "Katy," Nell called to me, "ask your mother can Peggy come out just for a bit. Mrs. Bishop said I could!" Nell had a bright pink scarf wrapped around her neck, and her cheeks were pink, too, from the cold. Paul scraped some snow from the porch rail and made as if to put it down her neck, and Nell shrieked, as he wanted her to, and hunched her shoulders against him, laughing. Paul often teased Nellie till she giggled and blushed. Once, in the fall, when she was hanging sheets on the line in their backyard, I saw Paul come up behind her and put his face suddenly right into her hair. He tickled her with his nose against her neck and slid his arm around her waist. She had to wrestle him away, but she was laughing.

"We'll go sledding!" Paul called to Austin and me.

"Bundle up," Mother said when I went in for Peggy, "and don't stay out too long. Peg, you bring her home by lunchtime, and see that your sister doesn't let that little Laura Paisley get too cold!"

"Or Austin," I reminded my mother. "Nell must watch out for him, too."

"Boys," Mother said, laughing. "Austin and Paul

57

can watch out for themselves, I imagine."

My friend Jessie Wood appeared at her corner, dragging her sled, and off we went, the group of us, to the hill beyond the Presbyterian church, pulling our sleds behind us, Laura Paisley perched on one and giggling as she bumped along. Everywhere were children and sleds in the new-rolled streets; and we could hear the jingle of sleigh bells as horses trotted by, pulling runnered cutters instead of the buggies that they were accustomed to. They tossed their heads and snorted steam.

"Did you go sledding when you lived at home, Peggy?" I asked. She was walking beside me, holding my hand.

"We didn't have sleds," she explained. "But we sat on cooking tins and slid down the hill. They whirled us all about."

"Nellie too? And Jacob?"

"Nellie did till she moved in to town. And once I held Anna in my lap and slid. But Jacob never, though he watched. I think he don't like the fast-ness."

"I don't, either," I confessed. "I just like the little hills."

"Katy's a fraidy-baby," Jessie said.

"No, I'm not," I replied, but I knew it was true that I was.

"Ride with me, Katy, and try the big hill," Peggy

58

offered. "I'll hold you tight, I promise. It's a treat, full-speed. And the boys, they'll call you scaredy-cat if you don't."

So I did. Peg was strong and sturdy, and I wasn't frightened with her arms tight around me. I sat in front of her, on her long wool skirt. She pulled the guide rope up on either side, put her feet firm against the steer board, and we pushed off and sailed, both of us shrieking laughter all the way to the bottom of the hill, where we had to turn sharp to miss a tree. Then we stood there and watched as the others came down: Austin on his own, belly-whopping, and Jessie, too, lying on her sled and laughing as she flew by. Finally Paul and Nellie flew past together with Laura Paisley wedged in between. But Laura Paisley was fearful and cried. So Peggy and I took her to the babies' hill and left Nell and Paul on their own.

On the gentle slope Laura Paisley wasn't fright-ened. Peggy sent her down again and again, and I waited at the bottom to haul her back up. From there, we could hear Austin hollering as he sped down the big hill, and I could see Jessie go just as fast and call out just as loud. Now and then we heard Nellie call out, too, in delight. Looking over from where I stood, I could see her bright pink scarf fly in the wind as Paul, behind her on the sled, steered the two of them down, slicing a turn at the bottom each time. The tree at the bottom loomed like a danger, but all the sledders knew how to make the turn at just the right instant.

"Push me!" Laura Paisley begged, so Peg would give her a gentle shove and watch as she slid slowly and then tumbled, giggling, from the little sled at the bottom of the gentle slope.

Going home for lunch, I think we were all like the horses, excited and prancing. Nell, especially, was like a wild thing let loose; she teased and shouted and her voice was so shrill that Peggy murmured "Shhhh" to her in embarrassment at what others might think. But Nellie turned away with an irritated shrug and went to walk with Paul. She didn't care what others thought.

6. JANUARY 1911

Nell came over to visit her sister late on a sleety Thursday afternoon. They both had Thursday off, and usually Peggy went to the library that day, often taking me with her; she said she didn't mind. Nellie always went to town, to the pictures or the shops.

But today it was too cold and wet to walk far. Nellie was in a foul mood when she came over. She pulled off her coat and boots in the kitchen and unwound the scarf from her thick, damp hair. She had had other plans, she said, but the weather made her plans fall through.

Together the sisters went up to Peggy's third-floor room. Sometimes Peg let me go up there and visit when she had free time, but I could tell she didn't want me tagging along now. She and Nellie were chattering about grown-up girl things, and from my room below I could hear Nell's whoops of laughter and Peggy's quieter, more serious voice.

"They want to be by themselves," I complained to Mother, feeling left out.

She was in the little room at the end of the upstairs hall, the one we called "the sewing room" though no one ever sewed there. Mother was at the pine table with an album open on it, and she was carefully pasting things in what she called a "memory book." It was where the postcard of Niagara Falls was, and the newspaper account of Mother and Father's wedding. A dried and flattened flower was attached to one page, with a note in Mother's careful penmanship describing a tea party where a vase of pink roses had been part of the decoration. It was hard to imagine the brown faded thing as one of those roses.

Mother listened for a moment to the noises from Peggy's bedroom. She smiled. "I'm glad we got the quieter of the Stoltz sisters," she said. "Mrs. Bishop says that Nellie's a good worker but she has a very frivolous side."

"What's *frivolous*?"

"Silly."

"I don't think Nell is silly. She's very serious about wanting to be in pictures."

Mother raised an eyebrow. I knew she disapproved of the pictures, and I was sorry I had mentioned it. "What's that?" I asked, and pointed at a wisp of hair gathered and tied with a ribbon and attached to the page.

"That's yours, Katy," Mother said, looking at it fondly. "You were two years old and I trimmed your hair. You didn't have a lot, but it was in your eyes until I snipped it back.

"And look at this!" She pointed to a picture. "You might remember this. You and Jessie Wood were both four that summer, and Jessie's father had a new camera."

I peered at the photograph of two solemn little girls, side by side, wearing hats, and gradually I remembered that day at the lake. It was summer. It came to me in fragments, in little details.

Jessie had black shoes, and mine were white.

The air smelled like pine trees.

A cloud was shaped like my stuffed bear. Then its ears softened and smeared, and it was just a cloud, really, not a bear at all (I knew it all along); then, quickly, the cloud itself was gone and the sky was only blue.

And there were fireworks! We were visiting at

the Woods' cottage there. Cottage sounded like a fairy tale: a woodcutter's cottage. Hansel and Gretel and their cottage.

But the Woods' cottage was not a fairy-tale storybook one. It was just a house. They invited my family to come to their cottage for the holiday called Fourthofjuly, which I didn't understand, and for fireworks.

I remembered the scent, the sky, the heat, the wide-brimmed straw hats we wore to protect our faces from the sun, and the white shoes and black. The shoes and stockings and dresses—even the hats—were removed, at some point, because my memory told of Jessie and me, wearing only our bloomers, wading at the edge of the lake. We chased tiny silvery fish—minnows! Someone told us they were called minnows, and we said that to each other, laughing: "Minnows! Minnows!"

After a while we were shivering, even though the day was hot. My fingertips were puckered, pale lavender. Our mothers rubbed us dry with rough towels. Jessie fretted because there were pine needles stuck to her damp feet. We played in the sand at the edge of the lake.

The parents sat on the porch, talking, while Jessie and I amused ourselves, still half-naked in the sunshine, digging with bent tin shovels in the damp sand. Jessie had a pail and I didn't. I pretended that I didn't care about her pail, though secretly I wished it were mine, with the bright painted picture printed on its metal side: pink-faced children building castles, green-blue water, foamed with white, curling behind them.

Stealthily I followed a beige toad that hopped heavily away into tall grasses edging the small beach. Soon I could no longer see the toad (I had begun to think of him as "my" toad) but when I waited, silent, I saw the grass move and knew that he had hopped again. I waited, watched. I followed where the grass moved. It was taller than my head, now, and I was surrounded by it and was briefly frightened, feeling that I had become invisible and not-there with the high reeds around me. But the world continued to be close by. I could hear the grownups talking on the porch, still.

"Where's Katy?" I heard my mother ask, suddenly.

"Jessie, where did Katy go?" Mrs. Wood called in an unconcerned voice.

"I don't know." Jessie's voice was not that far away from me.

"She was right there. I saw her just a minute ago." That was my father's voice.

"It's amazing, how quickly they scamper off, isn't it?" Mrs. Wood again. She was using a cheerful voice, but I could tell that now she was worried, and I was made pleased and proud by the worry.

"Katy!" My mother was calling now. "Katy!"

I should call back, I knew. But I liked the feeling of being concealed there, squatting in the moist earth, with the high grass golden above me. I liked hearing things happen around me, being an observer, but hidden. The breeze blew the grass and it closed above my head, creating a small, secret place where I fit. I had already forgotten my toad in the new excitement of being lost to the grownups. So I held still.

"You go that way, Caroline," my father said. "Check over there behind the woodpile and by the shed. I'll look in this direction."

"She wouldn't have gone into the house, would she? She would have had to pass us, to go into the house. We would have seen her. Katy!"

"Jessie, are you sure you don't know where she went?" Mr. Wood sounded angry, as if he were scolding his little girl.

Jessie began to cry. It pleased me somehow, that she was crying. She deserved to cry, because she owned a tin pail with bright paintings on its side.

"Katy! Katy!" My mother's voice was quite far from me now.

"Let's think." Jessie's mother said this. "*Hush, Jessie.*" (Jessie was still crying loudly.) "She wouldn't have gone far because she was barefoot. It's stony out there beyond the house. It would hurt her feet."

"Kaaaaty!" It was like a song in my mother's voice, when she called it that way. "Henry," she called to my father, "she isn't over this way."

"Everyone be absolutely quiet for a moment," Mr. Wood commanded. "She might be calling and we wouldn't hear her."

It was silent except for Jessie, who was now howling. In my mind, I scolded Jessie for not obeying her father. "Shhhh," Mrs. Wood said to her angrily, and finally Jessie was quiet.

Now, into that important silence, was when I should have called out. "Surprise!" I should have shouted. "Here I am!"

But I didn't. I waited. There was a bug near my toe, and I watched it waddle across the slick surface of wet earth. I put my hand near it and hoped that it would mount my finger and walk on me. But carefully it found a path around my hand. I began thinking very hard about the bug, and I forgot my family and their worry. I crouched there, and then lay down, slowly curling into the warm mud that was as soft and private as a bed. The sun was hot on my head and back, coming down through the curtain of grass that surrounded me, and things became dreamlike.

I woke when they found me, and now my mother was crying, so I was vaguely sorry that I hid. But I liked the attention. I was the heroine of the story, now: the little lost girl. *The one in danger.*

We were given cookies. Mrs. Wood must have made the cookies, because they had raisins in them, and my own mother knew that I disliked raisins. Meticulously I picked each raisin out and dropped it into the bushes beside the porch. My mother saw me doing this and smiled, creating a secret between us.

Then we were re-dressed. Jessie was upset still. I recognized her feeling, the feeling of being left out, overlooked, angry at things that you don't even understand, so that you cry in frustration and look for something to blame. *I should be the one crying!* I thought. *After all, I was the one who might have drowned, who might have been eaten by a bear!* Instead, I smiled, and it was Jessie who whined and made the grownups impatient. She wailed when her stockings were pulled on, worried that there may be pine needles—oh, yes! I understood, now! She was troubled by the word *needles*. The mothers, both of them, kept reassuring her that her feet were clean and dry. But it wasn't dirt or dampness that frightened her! It was *needles*!

Later there were the surprising bursts of color in the sky, and the alarming sound of the fireworks display. I curled up on my father's lap on the cottage porch, watching. I was sleepy, puzzled by the sounds and explosions of light, but not frightened. My father's shirt was soft against my cheek, and he smelled as he always did, father-smells of shaving lotions and shoe polish and pipe tobacco. (Mother was cologne and powder and the laundry starch ironed into her shirtwaist.)

I suppose Jessie was there on her own father's lap, but she was not part of my evening memory, which had grown small to enclose only my father and me. And mosquitoes. There were mosquitoes buzzing on the porch, and Father brushed them away from my bare arms and slapped at his own neck from time to time.

"Yes," I said to Mother, as we looked at the photograph together. "I do remember it."

From above, still, there came the sound of low voices murmuring. I looked again at the photograph of the two little girls, Jessie and me, and pretended for an instant that they were Peggy and Nell. One quiet and watching, tidy and careful. The other, banging a shovel against a bright tin pail. Eager. Brash. Impatient. Shrill.

7. FEBRUARY 1911

Winter dragged on, and soon enough we tired of snow. January came and went, and February. Mornings were still dark when I dressed for school in February, and the dark of evening came much too early. Father built a fire after supper and then while Pepper, the dog, slept on the rug, he read aloud to us in the parlor while Mother's fingers flew over her knitting. Upstairs, in a drawer, baby clothes were folded and waiting.

Peggy sat, sometimes, and listened. Upstairs, her room was very cold, and Mother said she should stay down in the warm parlor with us, evenings. So she took the dark green chair in the corner and mended. Father read *David Copperfield* and I saw Peggy cry a little at the sad parts.

In the afternoons Peggy read to herself while Mother napped. Once each week we went to the library, the two of us, and sometimes, if she promised to behave, Jessie came along.

Early one Friday evening the telephone rang, and Father was called away to the hospital. Mother sighed, set her knitting down, and took up the book. But her voice was different, and she didn't act the parts like Father did, using comical voices. Even she said so.

"I just can't do it as well," Mother said regretfully. "I hope he gets back early."

But Father was gone all night, and in the early morning came in smelling foul and went right upstairs for a bath. There had been a terrible fire at Schuyler's Mill.

"Some of the men are laying blame on the Stoltz boy," I heard Father tell Mother in their bedroom as he dressed. "Peggy's brother. He hangs about the mill often; he loves it there. And the men make fun of him because of his affliction. Now they're looking for someone to blame."

Mother's voice sounded very worried. "Might it be true?" I heard her ask. "Is he responsible? Oh, that would be terrible news to give Peggy."

"No, no. One of the late workers lighted a cigar

71

and the dust burst into flame like an explosion. People saw the whole thing. The Stoltz boy wasn't even there."

The entire mill was gone, they had told him, just the walls left standing, and the grindstone lying in the rubble. Men had come from everywhere to fight the fire and some of them were burned.

Father said at breakfast he hoped they would live but wasn't sure. He and other doctors had worked all that night. But when I asked him to tell me what it was like, and what the doctors did, both Mother and Peggy shushed me.

"It's bad for the baby to talk about such things," Peggy explained, taking me aside later that morning, when she was ironing. "It would upset your mama, and then the baby will be damaged."

"I don't see how. The baby's very cozy inside. It floats, Father told me, and swims."

"Babies can be marked," Peggy said in a serious voice. "I heard of a woman who was frightened by a runaway horse, and her baby was born with a mane and tail."

"Peggy!" I sputtered with laughter. "I *know* that can't be true! You didn't really see it, did you?"

"Well, no, but I heard."

"Someone was fooling you."

Peggy thought about it and smiled, finally. "Maybe," she admitted. "But it *is* true that you mustn't upset a mother-to-be. You know the boy who delivers the groceries from the market?"

"Yes." It was a boy from my school, actually, a sixth-grader named Edward, who brought the groceries in his wagon. My mother always gave him a nickel at the back door.

"He was marked on his face when his mother was carrying him. She likely saw something hideous and put her hand to her face in just that place."

Edward had a pale pink stain across his chin and cheek. "Father calls it a birthmark," I told Peggy.

"You see?"

I didn't, exactly, and resolved to ask Father more about it when we were alone together.

Peggy set the iron back on the stove to reheat. She folded the heavy sheet she'd been ironing, set it aside, and took another, damp and rolled, from the basket. The moisture and heat felt good in the kitchen with the cold weather outdoors.

"Peg? Is *touched* the same as marked?"

"Touched?" She looked at me, puzzled, as she laid the sheet out on the board.

"Jacob. You said he was touched."

The hot iron sizzled when she laid it on the sheet, and she moved it so that it wouldn't scorch.

Peggy chuckled. She looked fond. Always when she spoke of her brother, she got that fond look. "My mother says 'touched by the Lord,' and I think it's true.

"My pa, though, he don't think that," she confided. "He wishes he had him a boy who could take on the farm one day. Jacob can't ever."

"But you said he's good with animals." I had seen it, too, watching him with our own horses—for he had come many evenings now, and I had seen him there, in the stable—but I didn't talk to Peggy about Jacob's visits. It was not that they were wrong, or even secret, but they seemed private. "I've seen him with our horses, Peggy. It's almost as if he can speak their special language."

"He does have a way with animals," Peggy agreed. "But a farm is more than animals. There's the crops. The planting and the harvest. Taking care of the plow and the harnesses. Buying the seed. My pa has to go to the feed store and bargain and trade.

"And the butchering, too," she added. "It troubles my pa that Jacob runs and hides at butchering time. He feels them animals to be his friends. He can't be there when their time comes, and it angers Pa."

"But the kittens, Peggy! You told me about the kittens, when there are too many. You said Jacob is the one who—" I just couldn't say the rest.

She folded the ironed sheet and laid it on the pile. "Want to do your father's hanky?" she asked, picking up the small damp cloth from the basket.

So I took the hot iron and guided it across the square of linen. The iron was heavy, and it was not as easy as it looked, to get the handkerchief flattened perfectly and dry. Peggy helped me with her strong hand on mine.

"New kittens," she explained, "aren't the same as the kind you like to play with, all whiskers and fur and jumping around. Newborn, they don't seem like nothing lovable yet. Jacob does it quick and then forgets it, and even the mother cat don't seem to care.

"My land, look there in the corner of the hanky," she said, and ran her finger across the embroidered HWT. "His initials. I see that every time I iron, and think how wonderful it is to have your name be so important."

We heard a knock at the front door, and then Mother called from the hall.

"Katy! Jessie's here and wants to play!"

"Don't bring her in here, Katy," Peggy whispered. "She gets into everything and her hands are always dirty."

I laughed because it was true. Jessie Wood was my best girlfriend, but she was always a source of trouble. Mischief, sometimes, though I tried to steer her from it; and even if she wasn't into mischief, Jessie stumbled into things, dropped them, broke them, dirtied them. I left Peggy to the ironing and took Jessie up to my bedroom, where we could play with our paper dolls. Mother had given us last year's Sears Roebuck catalogue, and Jessie and I had made us a fine set of families from it. Now we were furnishing houses for them, choosing the furniture from the pages and making a life for our paper families. Jessie's was grand, with the most expensive suites and fancy wallpapers. But I had decided on a plainer life for mine, maybe on a farm, and I set about choosing overalls for the father, and a plow. I gave the little boy—I had cut him out the last time we had played—a pair of overalls, too; now I chose some sturdy shoes for him, so that when he roamed, as I thought he might, he would be warm and comfortable.

I made Jessie wipe her feet because it was thawing now, as February turned to March, and muddy in places where the snow was gone on the path. Then I made her wash her hands before we got the paper dolls out. Last time we played, I hadn't, and she got dirt smears on a fine Summer Leghorn Hat of Real Japanese Silk that she wanted for the lady in her paper doll family.

Jessie washed her hands, but she said our bathroom smelled peculiar.

And it was true. Peggy had taken Father's

clothes away, the ones he had worn all night at the hospital, but the smell from them remained. Peggy told me later it was the smell of burned people on him; she opened the window wide, though it was cold outside, and scrubbed the bathroom with carbolic acid.

It was only one week later that we heard the terrible, terrible news from New York. Peggy gasped and made a sound like "Oh!" when she heard at first, because her sister Nellie had been talking lately about New York, about going there to work and earn some money and maybe make her way into the pictures.

It was young girls like Nellie, and some even younger, who were working there and were caught in that terrible fire. From the eighth floor, the newspaper said, they jumped, some of them holding hands, their skirts and hair afire. Hundreds of them. Their bodies lay in heaps, smoldering, in the street. I thought of the smell of Father's clothes.

There was a list in our paper of all of them, the Mollys, Rosies, Annas, and even a Kate, my name, fourteen years old. Some of them weren't even identified; no one knew who they were.

One was only eleven, and her name was Mary.

In New York, thousands of people lined the streets in mourning for those working girls who wanted only to earn a better life for themselves. It was raining, and the newspaper picture showed thousands of umbrellas; I wanted to be there, holding a black umbrella, with rain dripping from the edge, and to bow my head as they were carried past, to the cemetery.

I was filled with a feeling of frustration at having no way to mourn for them. Finally, when no one was around to see, I went into Mother's room, opened her bureau drawer, and looked carefully through all of her ironed, folded shirtwaists. I was looking for a label that said TRIANGLE SHIRTWAIST COMPANY. I would tear it, scribble on it with ink, punish it in every way I knew.

But I found none there. Mother's clothes had been made for her, most of them, by Miss Abbott.

Instead, I made up a little prayer for Mary Goldstein, age eleven, who had died that day. I said it every night for several weeks. "Dear Mary Goldstein, please be happy in heaven and don't be frightened or on fire ever again, and now you can fly instead of falling." I murmured it every night before I went to sleep, adding "Amen" at the conclusion, so that God knew it was a prayer even though it hadn't been addressed to him.

8. MARCH 1911

"Please take me, Father!"

It was Saturday afternoon, so there was no school. Peggy had gone to visit her parents. Jessie was being punished for some mischief and was not allowed to play, and Austin was visiting his cousins in Harrisburg. Mother was resting upstairs. I was very bored.

The buggy was waiting, and Father was looking through his medical bag to be sure he had what he might need. We were in his office, and I watched while he added a small bottle of a white powder that he kept in the locked cabinet. The call summoning him had come just after lunch.

"You know I'm not a bother!"

He snapped the bag closed. "Of course you're not. Sometimes you're even a help, Katydid."

"Then may I come?"

"I won't be able to take you inside, Katy. It's not a patient's home, you know, where you can sit in the kitchen and wait. Not like the mill, where the men always thought it a fine thing that you were my helper. This is like a hospital."

"I won't mind. I can wait in the buggy. The horses will like me to do that. They get lonely waiting by themselves. And I'll take a book."

Father laughed. "All right. Let me just go tell your mother that you're coming along," he said.

And so, for the first time, an hour later, I found myself at the Asylum. I had seen it only at a distance before.

On the outskirts of town, the massive stone building was set in the center of expansive grounds surrounded by a wall with an iron gate. Carved deep into one of the stone pillars that formed the side of the gate were the letters that spelled ASYLUM, a word I could not have pronounced from sounding out the letters. Once, some time ago, when we drove past, Father had told me how to say it, and what it meant.

"I believe the dictionary would call it 'a place of protection,'" he had said.

"But who needs to be protected?"

"People who are ill and can't take care of themselves."

"So it's a hospital, really," I said.

"Yes. In a way."

"Jessie says it's for crazy people. She said imbeciles and lunatics and madmen."

Father smiled. "Those are just other words for people who are ill," he explained. "Ill in their minds. And at the Asylum, people take care of them."

"Jessie's afraid of it."

"No need," Father said.

"Jessie's afraid of bugs, too. I'm not." I felt quite smug.

But in truth, on this day, when the heavy gate was actually opened by the attendant in the gatehouse and Father drove the buggy inside the grounds, I did feel a little frightened. The building was so large—I counted five floors, and that was only in the central section; there were wings to the sides—and so silent.

Paths curved around the grounds, and benches dotted the landscape here and there, but on this late-March day no one was strolling or sitting outdoors. There was still leftover snow not yet melted, and the air was chilly. Father had wrapped a blanket around me and made me wear my mittens.

He tied the horses to the post in front of the building and told me he would not be long. If my feet got cold, he said, I should climb down and walk briskly until they warmed up. One good quick walk up and down the driveway, stamping hard with each step, would be a good treatment for cold feet. "Doctor Thatcher's prescription," he said to me, laughing.

Then he went up the granite steps, pulled the bell cord at the front door, which opened for him, and went inside.

I talked a bit to Jed and Dahlia, and I could see their ears flick back and forth, so I knew they were listening. Then I opened my library book and found the marker to show me where I had left off. It was a book I liked, *Mrs. Wiggs of the Cabbage Patch,* but it was hard to turn the pages with my mittens on, and too cold to take them off. I couldn't concentrate and tried reading aloud. Chapter 6, where the little Wiggs girls have their hair ironed on the ironing board, was very funny; I had read it once already, and it made me laugh, so I read that part again, to the horses.

But it didn't seem very funny a second time. The horses didn't listen, and my feet were cold, so finally I set the book aside and climbed down from the buggy to follow Dr. Thatcher's prescription.

Stamp, stamp, stamp. I marched like a soldier, and the man in the gatehouse came to his door to look at me curiously, then disappeared again inside the small building's warmth. I followed the edges of the building's shadow as it fell across the ground. The roof outline had sharp turnings where chimneys extended high into the air; and on this chilly day there was smoke coming from them, which made a wavery flicker on the snow. I followed the chimney outlines on my march, turning corners sharply as I knew soldiers did.

Once around the whole outline with all its turnings, and my feet had warmed, just as Father had said. I marched down the side wall back toward where the buggy was waiting. Then, through the marching song that I was humming half-aloud, I heard a scream. It sounded like a woman, but it was hard to tell.

The gateman did not put his head out again, though I knew he must have heard it.

The person screamed a second time, and then a third. It seemed to come from high up, from one of the upper floors. The windows were all tightly closed, and I could see bars across them. But the sound pierced the outside air as if it had come straight through the thick stone walls of the Asylum. The horses tossed their heads and snorted, and I stood by them and patted their noses and told them not to be frightened. But I was frightened myself.

I thought to run up the front steps, where my father had gone, and to pull the bell cord as he had done, so that someone would come and let me go inside, where he was. But inside was the scream, as well, and I did not want to be nearer to it. I stood by the horses, stamping my feet still from habit, and did not know what to do.

Then the door opened, and my father came back to me. Now everything was silent again. Father was carrying his medical bag as he always did, and when he saw that I was stamping my feet, he smiled at me and said I was a good patient to follow his directions.

"I heard a sound, Father," I told him when we were safely trotting on the road, outside of the iron gate and the stone pillar with its terrible carved word.

"A sound?"

"Somebody screaming. I could hear it right through the walls."

"Yes," he said. "It was a woman. I didn't know that the sound would go right outside. I'm sorry, Katy, that it frightened you. Sometimes the Asylum patients feel a need to scream. I don't know why."

"Is someone hurting them?"

"No, no. They're well cared for. They just seem

to be hurting inside their own heads."

"Can't you fix them? Isn't that why you came?"

He shook his head. "They called me because one of them had a bad stomachache. I can fix *that,* Katy. I've fixed tummyaches for you, haven't I, often enough?"

I nodded. "But the other can't be fixed? The inside-the-head part? The screaming part?"

"No. That can't be fixed."

"Do they *all* scream?"

Father held the reins in one hand and put his other arm around me. "You know, Katydid, there are one hundred and twenty-two patients in the Asylum right now. If they all screamed, we would hear it all the way on Orchard Street. It would blow our roof right off."

I knew he was trying to make me laugh. I didn't, though.

"Some of them never make a sound. They don't even move, those silent ones. They sit in the same position and stare into space, some of them for years," Father said. "Some walk back and forth, back and forth. One dances, all alone. Others sing, or talk."

"Or scream?"

"Or sometimes scream."

"Can't you give them medicine?"

He sighed. "You know a strange thing, Katy? Sometimes they are better if they have a high fever. So some doctors are trying to figure out ways to push their temperature up, as if they had malaria, or pneumonia. They've tried giving them sulphur and oil. But I think it's too dangerous. I think there must be another way."

I realized that he was talking to me as if I were grown up.

"I want you to find the way," I said. "I want you to fix those people."

"Someone will, one day," he said. "Maybe not me. But someone."

He jiggled the reins to hurry the horses. Behind us, the Asylum grew small in the distance. I tried to think of another sound to bury the memory of the scream. *Shoooda shoooda shoooda* came to my mind. I rubbed my mittened hands in circles on my coat and thought of Jacob.

9. APRIL 1911

Gram arrived from Cincinnati by train. She came every summer but this time it was earlier than usual; this time she came in April because of the baby. I had helped Peggy as she cleaned the big spare bedroom, the one with the pink-flowered wallpaper, that Gram always used on her visits. We laid the freshly starched and ironed bureau scarf on top of the tall bureau, and we set out the silver brush-and-comb set that Mother usually kept packed away in a drawer.

Miss Abbott had even put a new blue satin binding on the blanket for Gram's bed. I watched as

Peggy smoothed the crocheted coverlet over the blanket, and then we took a small pillow filled with pine needles and set it atop, for the lovely smell.

The curtains were freshly washed and starched and ironed. Naomi had baked an orange cake, and the house smelled of it. The brass knocker on the front door was polished. Everything seemed new and shiny, and it was in part, of course, for Gram, because she hadn't visited in a long time.

But I knew it was also for the baby. The baby would be coming very soon.

I went with Father in the buggy to meet the train, and there she was, wearing a hat and gloves as she stepped down with the conductor reaching up for her hand. The porter helped Father move her bags to the buggy, and I took Gram's hand and skipped beside her after she had distributed coins to all of those who had helped her on her journey. The conductor tipped his hat to her and said that he hoped she had a nice visit with her family.

Of course she said how I had grown.

The train blew its whistle and began to move slowly from the station—ours was a very short stop, being such a small town—on its way to Philadelphia beyond. I saw faces in the windows of the cars, and though they had watched with interest as Gram left the train with all of her things, I could tell that now their thoughts were moving on to their own destinations and whatever families, jobs, and vacations lay ahead for each of them.

"That's new paint there, isn't it, Katy?" Gram asked, pointing to a house on the corner. "I believe that house was gray on my last visit. And now look: it's sparkling white. Things change so when you've been away."

I nodded. "And, Gram," I told her, "there was a terrible fire at Schuyler's Mill. People were burned but no one died, Gram, because Father took care of them."

"The good Lord helped, I expect," Gram said.

"Maybe. But, Gram? *Colloidal silver.* That's what the doctors used. And tannic acid."

I could see Father smiling as he tapped the horses gently with the buggy whip and steered them toward home. "Katy aims to be a doctor when she's grown," he explained to Gram.

"I *never,*" Gram said. But she was smiling.

At home she hugged Mother, saying, "Caroline, Caroline," holding her carefully because of her size and the baby inside. "It won't be long, will it?"

Father took her coat and hat after Gram had carefully undone the hatpin that held it firmly on her gray hair. Peggy came from the kitchen, looking shy, and was introduced.

There were gifts: baby clothes, lovely things that Gram had embroidered herself; and for me, a book: *Elsie Dinsmore*. I had already read it from the library but didn't tell her that, and it was good to have it for my own, though in truth I didn't like the girl Elsie much. She seemed too good and had no spunk. Peggy thought the same; we had read it together.

Gram brought greetings from my mother's brother, Uncle James, and from Aunt Eleanor and the Cincinnati cousins. Gram lived at Uncle James's house, and I could tell that she didn't like Aunt Eleanor, though she was careful to say only nice things. There was always a little tone to her voice when she spoke of Eleanor, what a fine house she kept, and such a civic-minded woman.

Uncle James had been just a baby, and my mother only three years old, when my grandfather died. He took sick, she said, one morning, and was gone by nightfall, nothing anyone could do. For that reason Gram always wore a black ribbon around her neck, in mourning. The photograph we had of my grandfather showed him looking no more than a boy, though he was twenty-seven when he died. I wondered sometimes: if they were to meet in heaven, Gram and the young husband she still grieved for, might he still be that young boy and she a gray-haired lady with a mourning band around her neck, and a feathered hat held on by a pin? If so, I thought they would hardly have much to say to each other at all.

I loved Gram. She talked to me as if I were a grownup, and on earlier visits she had taught me card games (Naomi disapproved; her church thought playing cards were of the devil) using the playing cards that she always carried with her in her bag. She played something called patience, by herself, laying the cards out one by one on the table by the parlor windows.

When she went upstairs to freshen up, I followed along behind and took her down the hall to see the nursery with the baby clothes all waiting and the pink and white blanket Mother had knitted folded on the arm of the rocker.

"Mother and Father say they don't care, but I do hope for a boy," I confided to Gram.

"It's nice to have both," she said, nodding her head. "I remember being glad when James was born, to have a boy after a girl. But most of all, you hope for the baby to be healthy and strong."

"And not marked," I added. "Our grocery boy was marked on his face because his mother was frightened by something hideous and placed her hand just so." I showed her, with my hand to my chin.

Gram made a tsk-ing sound. "I'm sure your mother has taken very good care of herself," she said, "and your baby will be perfect. Whoever told you that about the grocery boy? Not your father, certainly."

"Peggy did."

Gram smiled. "She's a country girl. But I'm sure she's a great help to your mother."

"Oh, yes. Peggy works hard. And do you know what? Her sister's right next door. Do you remember my friend Austin Bishop, the boy with the pretty little sister named Laura Paisley? Peggy's sister Nell is a hired girl at the Bishops'."

"Two sisters side by side. Isn't that nice? Does Nell look like Peggy, with that thick brown hair?" Gram leaned forward to the looking glass and patted her own hair to tidy it.

"Not really. Nellie's hair is bright red, and she's more—" I tried to think of the right word to describe Nell: the overabundance of pink in her cheeks; her wild, flame-colored hair; the extra flounces in her clothing.

"More glamorous," I said, finally.

Speaking of Peggy's sister made me think, suddenly, of something uncomfortable I had seen in the Bishops' barn. I willed the thought from my mind and took my Gram's hand, to lead her down the hall again, back downstairs to the waiting dinner and the warm comfort of my family.

Austin came over on Saturday afternoon to play, and Peggy gave us cookies. We stood by Gram, watching her with the cards, and she tried to show us how the game went, but Austin was bored by it and so after a while we went outdoors.

Austin was in my class at school, but being a boy he played only on the boys' side of the playground while I played on the girls', and we never looked at each other during recess. But at home, on Orchard Street, we often played a game we had created together. We called it Tragedy and Disaster, and it took many forms.

On this early April afternoon, we played the version named San Francisco Earthquake. "Tragedy and disaster!" we called out together, and then shook the porch furniture until the wicker legs of the chairs thumped on the floor. We screamed, "Tremors!" again and again until Mother came to the door and told us to be quieter.

So we played Shipwreck, instead, sitting quietly in the porch chairs and commenting about the beauty of the sea, then tipping over and drowning silently after a few last words. "Tragedy and disaster!" we gulped. Pepper kept getting up from where he was sleeping by the steps to come sniff our bodies.

Then, because drowning wasn't very interesting after we had done it twice, we decided to be saved by a lifeboat. There had been a shipwreck off Nantucket a few years before, when a liner named *Larchmont* had collided with another ship. People had been saved by the lifeboats, though the ship was lost forever, and with it some treasure, or so it was said.

We found boards in the Bishops' barn, dragged them to my front yard, and arranged them just below the porch railing, though we were careful not to smash the budding azaleas, because I knew Mother would be cross if they were ruined.

We began the game again, seating ourselves very properly in the porch chairs that we had arranged side by side, imagining them to be on the deck of a ship.

"How do you do," I said to Austin, holding my fingers around an imaginary teacup. "What a lovely day it is."

"Yes," he replied. "How do you do. My name is Mr. Larchmont."

I kicked his chair and whispered, "You can't be. That's the *boat*'s name."

He puffed on an imaginary cigar. "They named this ship after me," he explained in a loud voice.

"Oh," I replied, sipping my tea. "How nice. And isn't it a lovely ocean? Such beautiful water."

"Yes indeed," he said. "But I believe I can see another ship coming dangerously close."

"I do hope it doesn't strike us."

"I'm sure it won't," Austin said. "Would you like to dance, or stroll?"

"Stroll," I decided. So he took my arm and we

walked slowly across the porch. He puffed some more on his cigar.

"Here it comes!" I called out. "Collision!"

"To the lifeboat!" Austin cried, and we scurried to the porch railing.

"Tragedy and disaster!" we shouted together. We climbed the railing, held hands, and jumped down onto our boards.

"I think it's supposed to be only women and children," I said, after we were afloat in the yard.

Courageously Austin said, "I'll make room for them." He leapt into the sea and prepared to drown.

"Wait!" I said. I jumped from my lifeboat and shook a branch of the nearby forsythia bush. Its few remaining yellow blossoms broke loose and fluttered down. "Treasure," I announced, and returned to my boat. "Falling into the sea."

"I drown surrounded by gold!" Austin shouted heroically. Then he added, "Also sharks." Those were his last words before he flopped over and was still.

I noticed that a splinter from the lifeboat boards had torn my stocking and scratched my leg. Bravely, ignoring my injury, I picked up a small stick and used it as a paddle, stabbing at the earth of my yard to propel myself to safety while Austin floated nearby, his eyes open, golden forsythia blossoms in his hair. Pepper once again lifted his head curiously and ambled down the porch steps, sniffing at us to see what was wrong.

"No dogs allowed in the lifeboat," Austin announced from where he drifted dead in the sea, so I shoved Pepper away and floated on alone.

10. APRIL 1911

"Katy, wake up!" Peggy shook my shoulders, and I opened my eyes. It was very early on a Sunday morning.

"I have a surprise for you!" she said, as I sat up and yawned. "Hurry and dress."

"For church? It's too early."

"No, not church." Peggy was getting my underclothes from the drawer.

"The baby! Has the baby come?"

"No—whatever made you think that? Here, stand up. I'll help you with your nightgown."

"I thought I heard something in the night." I

97

tried to remember, but it was blurred now. "Father was walking in the hall, I think. And I heard Mother's voice."

"You must have dreamed it."

She was right; it was as hazy as a dream and already disappearing from my memory the way a dream does.

"Look out the window. Levi has the horses hitched up. Your father called him to come."

I glanced down and it was true. The buggy was waiting in the driveway beside the house, and Levi was there holding the harness reins. Jed and Dahlia stood patiently. The neighborhood houses were silent. The sun was just rising. The light was pink.

"Are we going someplace? It's Sunday. I'm supposed to go to Sunday school. These are the wrong clothes." She was buttoning my dress, an old one that I wore for play, not even to school, because it was faded and patched. Then she held up a pinafore and directed my arms through. "These are *play clothes,* Peggy."

"We have a vacation today," she said, and pulled the brush deftly through my hair. "Now go into the bathroom and wash your face and brush your teeth. Be quiet. Don't wake your mother."

I thought I could hear Mother and Father stirring in their bedroom, behind the closed door, but I obeyed Peggy. I was quick and quiet, and then I hurried down the stairs and was surprised to find that we were not even stopping for breakfast. Peggy had a basket packed already with toast and jam, which she said we would eat in the buggy. I drank a glass of milk quickly, put on my jacket, and we were off.

Off to the Stoltzes' farm! Peggy said we were going to visit her family.

She took the reins and to my surprise she could manage the horses as well as Father or Levi. She chuckled to find that I was surprised.

"I'm a farm girl, Katy!" she reminded me. "Eat your toast now so you won't be hungry. My ma will give us breakfast but it'll be awhile."

"Why don't we take Nellie, too? She could come, and Austin."

"Just us," Peggy said. "Nellie doesn't like the farm. She's too fancy, she thinks, for farms. And Austin? He's still asleep. It's just us today, Katy."

We had already passed the Bishops' house and moved down our quiet street; soon we were on the main street headed out of town. It was so early that no one was out.

"Want some toast?" I handed Peggy a half a slice of the toast smeared with blackberry jam.

She took it and nibbled. "Nellie never goes home," she said. "It really frets my ma."

"Never? But she has her days off, like you! All hired girls do!"

Peggy shrugged. "She finds other things to do. You know she goes to the pictures."

"She should go to the library instead," I decided aloud, but Peggy scoffed at the thought.

"Really," I insisted. "She never does, and she might like it. She could go with us. We could stop afterward at Corcoran's and have a ginger beer, with straws."

I loved drinking straws. And Corcoran's served tea biscuits, too. It was a treat to go there after the library.

Peggy clucked at the horses to remind them to lift their feet. "Nellie don't like to read," she said. "Even in school, she never did."

"Your sister Nellie doesn't like to, and your brother, Jacob, can't," I pointed out. "Isn't that strange?"

Peggy smiled and agreed that it was strange.

"Will Jacob be home?" I asked her.

"I expect so." She glanced at the sun, still low against the horizon. "He'll be helping my pa with the milking now. And by the time we get there, the milk will be in, and we'll have it still warm, on oatmeal. And honey with it, from the hives."

The thought made my cold toast unappetizing, and I threw the crust of it from the buggy to the side of the road, for birds and chipmunks to have.

"Do they know we're coming?"

"Yes. I telephoned."

"Do they mind, your bringing me?" I asked.

"Of course not," Peggy replied. "And when they find what a good girl you are, they may even want to keep you for their own!"

I glanced at her quickly because the thought made me a little fearful, but I could see she was teasing, and so I laughed as well.

I had not been inside the Stoltz farmhouse before. Peggy's mother greeted me warmly and hung my jacket on a wall peg.

"You're hungry, I expect," she said, and led me to the kitchen, where a wooden table was covered with a flowered cloth. The wood stove was hot, and kettles simmered atop it. The little girl—I remembered her name was Anna—sat in a high wooden chair and banged a spoon on the table. She smiled at me, then lowered her eyes, bashful.

The back door thumped open suddenly and Mr. Stoltz came in, with Jacob behind him. They smelled of barn, of hay and cows. Peggy's father set a bucket on the shelf beside the stove. Then he nodded at me and said, "Miss." He began to wash his hands, pumping the water with the handle at the sink. "Wash, boy," he said, and Jacob joined him.

It surprised me that Jacob did not look at me, or nod, or smile. I had thought that we were friends, in an odd but special way. Again and again I had stood with him in the stable, stroking the horses' massive heads side by side. We had never talked. Indeed, I had never heard Jacob speak. But we had made sounds together—I thought of it as our special kind of singing, there in the stable—and sometimes I had walked beside him and his dog for a way, through the alley behind our house, when he left to roam off to other places that I did not know about.

But Jacob did not look at me.

We sat around the table on sturdy wooden chairs. "Cap," Mr. Stoltz said, looking at his son meaningfully. Jacob turned his face away and pretended not to hear..

"Remove your cap, boy." When he repeated it, his tone was stern. Reluctantly Jacob grabbed the cap from his own head, exposing uncombed, curly hair. He held the cap crumpled in his lap.

Then we bowed our heads while Peggy's father asked the blessing. Even little Anna bowed her head, but I saw her peeking.

Mrs. Stoltz served us oatmeal and honey, as Peggy had promised. The cream was thick and golden, still warm from the cow.

"Did you milk the cow, Jacob?" I asked, feeling shy.

"Sure, Jake milks," Mr. Stoltz said.

To my surprise, Jacob began to make a rhythmic

102

sound: not the *shoooda, shoooda* of the millstone, not the song of the horses, but a *psssss, psssss* that he repeated again and again. Anna giggled.

"Enough, boy," his father said sternly. Then to me he explained, "That'd be the sound of the milk into the pail."

Peggy helped her mother wash the dishes, after, but they wouldn't let me, though I offered. Instead I played at the table with Anna. I folded and rolled the napkins into dolls, and we walked them around and made them say hello and goodbye to each other, with bows and curtsies that made the little girl laugh. She climbed down from her chair after a moment, ran off into another room, and came back carrying her own doll to show me. It was sewn of rags, with hair made from yarn and two buttons on it for eyes. I could tell it had been loved. Parts were worn and frayed from holding and, even as she showed me, Anna put her thumb into her mouth and began to stroke the doll in the way little ones do when they are tired. Then she giggled again and set the doll aside in her father's chair.

Mr. Stoltz and Jacob, with his cap firmly back in place, had gone back outside. "We'll water your horses," Mr. Stoltz had said, and I was glad that Jacob would be caring for Jed and Dahlia, who knew him well by now.

Peggy showed me around the little house: the

parlor, with its stiff chairs and worn rug. Back home, in town, we used our parlor every night, sitting there to read, or sometimes Mother played the piano. Gram played Patience in the parlor, and the fire crackled in the fireplace on chilly nights. But this room was cold and unused. The kitchen was the warmth of the Stoltz farmhouse.

Jacob slept in a tiny room behind the kitchen, and upstairs were two cold bedrooms, one that Peggy and Nellie had shared—it was Anna's now—and the other where their parents slept. I shivered and Peggy laughed. "It's spring now," she pointed out. "In winter it's *really* cold! But see? The comforters are stuffed with down. They're warm enough."

I felt the softness of the down-filled bedding. The rooms were dark, their walls bare of decoration, and the floors were splintery wide boards. No rugs; no flowered wallpaper; no silver-backed brush and comb.

"Where is the bathroom?" I whispered.

Peggy pointed through the window to the privy behind the house.

"Peg," her mother said as we passed through the kitchen on our way outdoors, "Floyd Lehman asked when you was to be at home. You want I should tell him? There's a telephone at the Fosters' now, and they'd call him to it."

Peggy blushed and said no. It was the first I knew that she had an admirer.

When we went outdoors, the spring air was warmer now than the early morning had been. Birds sang, and flowers were coming into bud, curled pink and white. A chipmunk ran across a stone wall and jerked its tail before disappearing into a chink. Anna trotted behind us as Peggy walked with me down to see the creek.

The water was deep. It moved past, swirling and foaming lazily around the rocks. Peggy held tight to Anna's hand as the little girl leaned forward curiously to see. We threw in some pebbles and watched the circles they made. A familiar-looking dog, brown with a white face, appeared, running toward us through some nearby tall grass, and Peggy stroked its head and spoke to it.

"It's Jacob's dog," she said, but I knew it already. The white-faced dog with floppy ears always sat by our stable and waited when Jacob was there, and then followed him when he left.

"He raised it from a puppy," Peggy explained. "Its mother died when she had a litter, and all the pups died but this one. We didn't even know for a long time. Jacob hid it in the barn and fed it cow's milk, dipping a rag in so the puppy could suck. Pa said he probably had to do it ten times a day, to keep the pup alive."

I looked down at the dog. It was sitting, now, in the grass beside Anna. Its tail wagged and it looked back at me with huge dark eyes.

"Does it have a name?"

Peggy chuckled. "Jacob don't name things," she said. "We all just call it Pup."

"Good Pup," Anna said solemnly, and patted the dog's back.

"Go find Jake!" Peggy said to the dog, and immediately it rose and trotted toward the barn. We followed. "I'll show you the animals," Peggy said.

"Lambs!" Anna announced. She ran ahead.

"Yes, there are new lambs. They always come at the end of winter. And there's a calf."

I followed Peggy into the cool darkness of the barn. For a moment it seemed silent inside, but then I began to hear the stirring of animals: the thump of shifting feet, the swish of a tail, the deep breath of living creatures. A sudden snorting grumble nearby startled me, and Peggy laughed when I jumped in surprise. She pointed to a penned area near the barn door, and I saw the huge pig, with its whiskery face, inside.

In another pen, lambs stood quietly next to their thick, silent mothers.

One mother had two little ones; I pointed and whispered, "Twins," to Peggy. But she shook her head.

"Sometimes they do have twins," she said. "But

these aren't. The small one? Its ma wouldn't take it when it was born. Sometimes that happens. The ma just turns away and wants nothing of it. And the lamb would die, too, with no ma to suckle it.

"But Jacob took this one and put it with this ma, since she had milk for her own, and coaxed her till she would feed it with the other. And now she does. See?"

As I watched, the smaller lamb nudged at the mother with its head and searched under her until it found milk.

"It's runty because it was awhile till she took it for her own," Peggy explained, "but it will grow now."

Mr. Stoltz appeared, wiping his hands on a rag, and he took Anna by the hand. "We'll go feed the hens," he said to his little girl, and she walked beside him happily off to the hen house on the other side of the barnyard.

"Jacob's above," Mr. Stoltz called back to Peggy and me. "He's waiting for the girl."

The girl? I thought he must mean me. Peggy's face confirmed it. She was smiling at me. "You'll have to climb," she said.

"I can climb. I climb with Austin all the time. We can go to the very top of the apple tree," I told Peggy.

She pointed down to the end of the barn, where a ladder led up to a dark hay-fringed opening.

107

"He's up there," she said.

"Why is he waiting for me?"

"He has something to give you," Peggy explained.

The cows shifted where they stood, as I passed them.

"Jacob?" I called from the bottom, though I knew he wouldn't answer. "It's Katy! I'm coming up!"

The ladder slanted and wasn't difficult to climb. Hay caught on my stockings and itched, and I knew it must be in my hair as well. It made me sneeze. I pulled myself up rung after rung until I reached the top and climbed into the loft. It was warm there, thick with bundled hay, and Jacob was standing by an opening in the wall so that light from the spring day was on him. Though he didn't look at me, I knew he knew I was there. He hadn't looked at me during breakfast, either, but I had felt that he followed every spoonful of oatmeal to my mouth. There was an awareness to Jacob's being.

He was looking, from under his familiar cap, out at the meadow behind the barn, toward the creek.

"Peggy and I went down to the creek with Anna and Pup," I told him. "It's beautiful today."

He didn't turn.

"Thank you for watering Jed and Dahlia."

He stared down at the meadow.

"Peggy pointed out your family's horse, in the pasture. She said his name is Punch. That's a nice name for a horse." I thought perhaps to express my sympathy, because Peggy had also told me that Judy, the other horse, had died not long before. But it was hard to express something of that sort to a person who looked away.

I waited. Finally I said, "Peggy told me you have something to give me."

He rocked back and forth a little. I had seen him do it before, a motion that I knew by now meant that he was pleased. Finally, he hummed a little— that was no longer a surprise to me, either—and he pointed down into the hay near his own feet.

I saw it then, and knelt down and picked up a small kitten the same color as the hay. Though small, it wasn't newborn; its eyes were wide open, dark brown, and when I stroked its soft golden fur, it began to purr.

Jacob rocked and rocked with pleasure.

"Oh, Jacob, thank you!" I said to him. "You knew I wanted a kitten, didn't you? Peggy must have told you." He looked away, back out toward the meadow, but his face was flushed with embarrassed excitement.

"Peggy!" I called down from the loft into the barn where she waited. "Jacob gave me a kitten!"

She came halfway up the ladder. "I know," she said. "He's pleased, doing it.

"Jacob?" she called gently to her brother. "You made Katy very happy."

"Thank you, Jacob," I said again. Then I lifted the kitten away from where it was cuddled against me, pulling its tiny claws loose from my pinafore. I leaned down and handed it to Peggy so that I could use both my hands on the ladder. At the bottom, I took it back from her and held it against me, feeling it purr.

"It's prettier than most," Peggy said, looking carefully at it. "He must have chose it for that.

"You'll have to give it a name," she said. "Jake don't, but you should."

I nodded. "But not yet. The right name will come."

At the midday meal (at home we called it Sunday dinner) there was chicken roasted so the skin was crisp, all manner of vegetables from the farm, and thick bread. We sat at the same table and bowed our heads again for the blessing, and when I peeked down to my hands in my lap, I could see the kitten sleeping there. Peggy had pinned up the corners of my pinafore to make a kind of carrying sack, and my kitten had been there the entire morning.

The telephone rang several times, and each time the whole family jumped; it was new to them, and they weren't used to it yet, and had to count the rings. Their ring was four-two, Peggy explained. That meant four long rings and two short, and they should answer.

Each time it rang, we all stopped talking, and counted. "One-three," Mrs. Stoltz said. "That's the Fosters." And later: "Two-two. That's for Mr. Ledbetter at the feed store. He won't be there on a Sunday."

Then, suddenly, while we were eating a dessert of apple brown Betty with cream poured over, the telephone rang four-two. At home I always answered and said, "Dr. Thatcher's residence," politely, but of course this was their home, not mine.

Mrs. Stoltz, looking a little nervous, picked up the earpiece from the box on the wall. "Stoltz," she said loudly, leaning over to speak into the box.

"Oh my, yes," she said, after a minute. "Yes, she's right here." She glanced over at me. "We've had a lovely time with her. Yes, I'll tell her that."

She began to hang the earpiece back on its hook, then looked confused, listened again, and finally said "Goodbye" uncertainly into the telephone. "My land," she said to us, laughing. "I'm not used to it yet."

She sat back down. "That was your pa, Katy. He said it's time for Peg to take you home."

Back home on Orchard Street, the house was very quiet. I took my kitten into the kitchen, poured him a small bowl of milk, and watched him lap it with his tiny pink tongue. He sneezed, after.

Peggy put away the food that her mother had sent. Then she found me a box as a home for the kitten, and I placed him there atop a pile of rags, and he fell asleep again.

"Now let's go see what your mama has been up to, and your Gram," she said. "They must be upstairs."

To my surprise, my mother was in her bed, propped up against the pillows. She was smiling. Gram sat nearby in a rocker, doing her embroidery, and, between them, in the bassinet, was the new baby.

"A little sister," Mama said, for I wouldn't have known from just looking. The baby had only a bit of hair, and her eyes were closed tight. She was wrapped in blankets.

I reached in and touched her nose with the tip of my finger, but she didn't stir.

"Where's Father? Does he know?"

"Of course. He was right here when she arrived. He's over at the hospital now, to check on some of his patients. But he'll be back and we'll all have supper together, up here in my room. Won't that be an adventure?"

"I'll set a table up," Peggy said. "And I can bring

the supper up on trays. My ma sent you a pot of vegetable soup, and some pie."

I was still examining what I could see of the baby. She was surprisingly pink. "When you unwrap her, can I see the rest?" I asked.

"Of course," Mother said, laughing.

"Does she have a name yet?"

Mother nodded. "Her name is Mary," she said.

Then I knew at once what the kitten's name was to be. It had to do with the girl who died in the factory, and the fact that I would not need to say my special prayer anymore. "Dear Mary Goldstein, please be happy," I said to myself for the final time. A new Mary was alive. And so was Goldstein, though he was sleeping in his box, with milk still wet on his whiskers.

11. MAY 1911

I sat at the kitchen table after supper one evening
with a pencil and paper. Naomi had just left, and
Peggy was finishing the dishes. Upstairs, Mother
was nursing the baby. Mary was a month old now,
but still she seemed to want to eat many times
each day. Mother didn't mind. She said it was a
nice relaxing time, there in the rocker with the
baby in her arms.

"Look here, Peggy," I said to her, and she leaned
over my shoulder to see where I pointed. I had
printed two names, one below the other.

KATHARINE THATCHER
AUSTIN BISHOP

"Now, I cross out all the letters that match. See, first the A, because there's an A in Austin. I put a line through both of them. Then the two Ts."

Peggy watched as I crossed out all the matching letters. "Now you say this to all the letters that are left: 'Love, Hate, Friendship, Marriage. Love, Hate, Friendship, Marriage—"

I examined the results. "Friendship. Good. At first I did it using Katy instead of Katharine, but that way it came out to be Hate.

"Now I'll do you," I told her. "What is his name? Floyd Lehman? You'll have to tell me how to spell it."

"No, I never." But she was laughing, and I knew she wanted me to.

PEGGY STOLTZ
FLOYD LEHMAN

"This is just foolish," Peggy said, but she helped me strike through the matching letters. *"Hate?"* She looked surprised at the outcome. "Maybe we should do like you did with your name, Katy. My real name is Margaret Ann."

This time, using Margaret Ann, it turned out

better and made Peggy blush. "Marriage," I teased her. She crumpled the paper and threw it away.

"Now we could do Nellie. I know who *she's* sweet on." I put my pencil to a fresh sheet of paper.

"Who?" Peggy looked genuinely puzzled.

"Paul Bishop," I told her slyly.

"No!" She was shocked, I could tell. "Don't say that, Katy."

"It's true."

I had thought that I would tell her what I had seen. But it was clear that she was truly troubled by the thought. So I stayed silent, and put my paper away.

I had never really paid much attention to Peggy's sister. She was always busy. Nell had come to work for the Bishops when Laura Paisley was born, and there was so much washing when you had a little one in the house. I knew that from my own house, now, where Peggy was busy every day with Mary's diapers and little gowns.

Austin called Nell "Nellie-Nellie-Jelly-Belly," just to torment her, and she swatted him lightly with her hand when he did; but you could tell she didn't really mind. She knew she was pretty and had a nice shape.

She was a hard worker, as Peggy was. But she had a different attitude to her, something I could sense, even though I was so young. You always felt that Nell had other things on her mind, things beyond the Bishops' house, things beyond Orchard Street, even beyond our town.

Watching Peggy, at our house, hanging the laundry on the line or washing up the breakfast dishes, you saw that she was always admiring the little things—the flowered dishes, Mother's lace-trimmed shirtwaists, Father's monogrammed handkerchiefs—that she hadn't had at her own home. She snapped the corners on the wet pillow slips before she pinned them to the line, and when she straightened them in the sun she sometimes ran her finger over the embroidered edges. She was careful, too: not from nervousness but from admiration. "I always do the little cream pitcher separate," she said to me once, as she washed the dishes. "See the gold on its edge? You don't want to chip that against something. It's too pretty, too precious."

(I had whispered it to Mother once, that Peggy loved the cream pitcher especially, and could we maybe get her one for Christmas. But Mother smiled and said that Peggy had no need of a cream pitcher, not until she got married. For Christmas we gave her warm gloves.)

But Nell, next door, though she did her work energetically and in good spirits, had no real interest in babies, dishes, or embroidery. She was simply biding her time. She was saving. Waiting. Her mind was on the future. Her heart was set on becoming Evangeline Emerson of the pictures.

On her Thursdays off, she never went to the library as Peggy did. She went off to town, swinging her purse, and Peggy had told me that sometimes she put paint on her face and met fellows.

"Maybe there will be a wedding," I suggested to Peggy, "and you can be bridesmaid. Sisters always are. What color bridesmaid dress would you like to have? I'd choose pink."

But Peggy shook her head. "No wedding," she said. "She only lets them take her to the pictures."

I didn't tell Peggy, but I was a little shocked by Nellie's interests. The nickelodeon was new in our town, and though I had heard about it from friends at school, I had never known anyone who went there. Mother said it was low-class, probably a little dangerous, and certainly not for children. Peggy had told me her sister wanted to look like Mary Pickford. Though I had heard the name, I had no idea, really, who Mary Pickford was until on Main Street, one day, I saw that the nickelodeon was showing a picture called *The Message in the Bottle*. WITH MARY PICKFORD, AMERICA'S SWEETHEART, the poster said, and displayed a picture of a pretty girl with long curls. She looked just Nellie's age. But girls that age, I thought, should be in school, learning geography and elocution. Not in pictures.

And certainly not in a burning shirtwaist factory like the other Mary, I found myself thinking as I stared at the pretty face in the poster and thought about the ways the lives of girls might go. Father had already explained to me that not many women became doctors, and those who did might have a hard time of it. He had known a girl in medical school, he said, and the other students—even Father, though he was ashamed of it now—had played some cruel tricks on her, to see whether she had the stuff for medicine. And she did. She ignored their pranks and became a doctor. But she never married, Father said, and never had children, which was a loss, he felt, to a woman.

I decided I could do it all, and would. I would go to college. Then I become a doctor and I would marry Austin Bishop and have children one day, and maybe would travel, too. I thought I might go to Africa and China and all the places we studied in school.

Austin's father, Mr. Bishop, had a new camera, much fancier than the one that Jessie's father had, and probably very expensive, my mother had told me. Austin's mother said it was foolishness.

But his father was fascinated with anything mechanical. He was the one who had built Austin's driving machine, the thing that I had once called the mazing, being little then, and foolish. The driving machine was gone now, for Austin was older and had a real bicycle, which he used to deliver papers up and down our street.

Mr. Bishop had been the first to have a writing machine, called a typewriter, in his office. His secretary had taken lessons and learned to operate it. So when he bought a Delmar folding camera and all the equipment to make pictures, Mrs. Bishop pretended to be astonished and exasperated, but we all knew she wasn't, really. She was used to Mr. Bishop and his fondness for machines.

One Sunday afternoon in May, when the sun was shining, he brought the camera out to the backyard and attached it to its tripod so that it stood there like some strange three-legged creature.

"My land," Nell said, and began smoothing her red hair with her hand. She was sitting on the steps holding Laura Paisley, but Laura Paisley, who was almost three years old, wiggled from Nell's lap and scampered toward the camera.

"Don't let that child touch anything!" Mr. Bishop ordered. But by then Laura Paisley had spotted Pepper, my dog, whom she loved, so she chased after him instead.

"I don't suppose it takes moving pictures, does

it?" Nell asked, watching Mr. Bishop set things up.

Paul was there. He often wasn't. Paul liked to be off with his friends, and sometimes his mother complained that she had no idea what that boy was doing, or who his companions were, and she feared for him. He was already enrolled for Princeton, where his father had gone, but if he didn't do well in his high school studies, Mrs. Bishop said, Princeton wouldn't want him for a nickel.

Now, teasing Nell, Paul knelt and pretended to be an actor, waving his arms around in a dramatic way before the camera. He made as if he were proposing to her. "Marry me and come to Paris!" he said in a dramatic voice.

I noticed Peggy watching Paul and her sister. She had been standing quietly with me, beside the flower garden, both of us interested but a little shy. Laura Paisley was frolicking with the dog, and Austin was chasing them both, carrying a ball he wanted to throw for Pepper to fetch. Baby Mary, bundled in blankets, was sleeping in her carriage, parked in the corner of the yard under a tree. Our mothers were on the porch, talking to each other, not really listening as Mr. Bishop gave out important information about the camera: "Now this Delmar has a ground glass focusing screen, and a Bausch and Lomb lens. That's the very best." If my father had been there, he would have paid

121

attention. But Father had been called to tend a patient.

I could see Peggy bite her lip when Paul did the acting in front of Nell. I could see she was embarrassed and hoped that her sister wouldn't encourage it.

I knew it was true, though, what I had told Peggy, that Paul and Nell were sweet on each other. I knew it for a fact. I had come on them—this had been some months before—in the early evening, in our stable, which could be reached from the Bishops' yard by a break in the hedge. I had heard the horses stir and stamp, and I thought perhaps Jacob might be there, as he so often was.

But when I slipped through the partly opened door, I saw it wasn't Jacob at all, but Paul and Nellie standing close together. I thought they were holding hands, but when I entered they pulled apart. Paul explained quickly that they had come over to borrow some harness oil. It looked like rain, he said, and they wanted to waterproof some old harness so it wouldn't crack. He turned and picked up the can from the shelf. Nellie didn't say anything. She looked flushed and nervous.

At first I thought it quite romantic and was glad I was part of their sweet secret now. From time to time I saw the two of them together, sometimes simply talking on the porch, and once on the corner near the grocery store, as if Paul had happened by as Nellie was starting home.

But my knowledge of their romance turned uncomfortable after I came on them in the Bishops' barn one afternoon when I was looking for Austin and thought he might be hiding from me. When I opened the barn door I could see right away that Austin wasn't there. But I heard a sudden frantic whispering from the corner where the hay was kept, so I went there without thinking, to see who it was and why they were hiding. They drew apart quickly, and Paul stood up. Nellie turned her back to me as if to fix her clothes. Paul was angry and told me to get lost. Nellie just looked away. There was hay caught in her red hair. Her apron was untied and her shirtwaist had come loose from her skirt.

My feelings changed then, though I wasn't sure why. It no longer felt romantic. Now it felt wrong and dangerous.

And by that day, the day of the camera, I felt that I didn't like Austin's brother. I had never paid much attention to Paul and his antics before, not really, though I had heard his mother complain to mine that he was wild. He wasn't being wild that day, just foolish, and I could see that Nell enjoyed it and was flattered.

But I could see, also, what she didn't: that he was mocking her in a cruel and secret way.

"Who's first?" Mr. Bishop called suddenly, interrupting everyone but Laura Paisley and Pepper. The two mothers went right on talking on the porch.

"Me!" Austin shouted. Secretly, I wanted his father to take my picture, but I could never shout like that.

But Mr. Bishop paid no attention to Austin at all. He turned toward Nell and Peggy, now side by side next to the garden with its early spring flowers. In their Sunday church clothes, they were as colorful as Mrs. Bishop's tall tulips.

"Ladies?" Mr. Bishop said. "Let's have a photograph of the two lovely sisters."

Even Nell, usually so sure of herself, turned a little shy. She and Peggy were silent, but they reached out and put their arms around each other's waists. Then they smiled toward Mr. Bishop. "Hold still," he said, and squeezed the bulb attached to his large camera. I watched as they stood, arms linked, holding still. Nell was taller, almost womanly, and her dress was more grown up. Peggy still looked like what she was: a very young girl with a ribbon in her hair. With his black folding box and its magical lens, Austin's father captured the two of them in that moment when the sun was shining and they had dreams, still, and thought that their lives could be what they shaped.

I have that photograph today, for Mr. Bishop gave us a copy of it. When I look at it, I am aware that it was the last time, that day in the Bishops' garden, that all of us were together and happy.

12. JULY 1911

Father took me with him in the buggy when he went to check on Mrs. Shafer's newborn twins, and he let Jessie go along this time. She and I sat one on either side of Father.

"Look!" I said to Jessie, and pointed, as we approached the Stoltz farm, which we had to pass on our way to the Shafers'. "That's Peggy's house! And Nellie's. That's where they grew up. They shared a bedroom on the second floor, but now it belongs to their sister, Anna."

"I wish I had a sister," Jessie said, frowning.

"Even a little baby one like you have would be better than none at all."

"Maybe someday you will," I suggested.

Jessie rolled her eyes. "My mother says absolutely not." I could see my father smile at that.

"Oh, look! Can you slow the horses, Father?" We were passing the large field beside the Stoltz farmhouse, and I could see Mr. Stoltz working his rig in the field, and Jacob behind him, helping.

"It'll be a good year for them," Father said. "They'll get a second hay crop in, with the first one this early."

"That horse's name is Punch," I told Jessie. "Peg told me, the day that she took me to the farm and her brother gave me the kitten."

"Punch? What kind of name is that?" Jessie wrinkled her nose.

"They had a Judy, too, but she died. Punch and Judy."

"Is that boy Peggy's brother?" Jessie asked, looking toward the field.

"Yes. His name is Jacob. He's almost fourteen." I waved to Jacob. "He's a good friend of mine," I added, feeling important to have such a friend, a half-grown boy. Austin played with Jessie and me, but older boys ignored us; or worse, like Paul Bishop, they made fun, and called us babies.

Father slowed our own horses and tipped his hat to Mr. Stoltz, who looked over and nodded without slowing his work.

Jacob seemed to be looking at us but did not wave back or nod his head the way his father had. Mrs. Stoltz and Anna were nowhere in sight, and I thought they must be in the house. There was washing on their line. Back at our house, in town, there was washing on our line, too. Peggy had been up early that morning, doing laundry.

Father jiggled the reins and the horses trotted ahead.

"We have more laundry than they do," I commented, "because of Mary. What a chore a baby is."

Father laughed. "Wait until you see what things are like at the Shafers' house, with those twins just born. You'll be glad we have only Mary to tend."

The Stoltz farm was slipping out of sight behind us. I shaded my eyes with my hand, looked back, and could see Jacob still, cap clamped on his head.

"He didn't even wave at you," Jessie commented. "I thought you said he was your friend. If I saw a friend go past, I would wave. I would call out 'Hello!' and I would watch and watch until my friend disappeared down the road. I would be waving the whole time."

"Well, Jacob forgets his manners," I explained, trying to excuse him.

Father chuckled. "The Stoltz boy is somewhat different, Jessie. He does things his own way."

"Very talented, too," I added, to impress Jessie. "He can do imitations of almost anything. He's probably making the clickety-clickety noise of that hay cutter right now. Don't you think so, Father?"

"I expect so. It's quite a feat, to imitate sounds the way he does."

"Listen!" Jessie commanded. "I can imitate a chickadee." She began to make the *chick-a-dee-dee-dee* sound over and over. I could even see the horses twitch their ears a bit. They were accustomed to me and Father and our quiet talk. But Jessie called out, imitating different birds, and wiggled in her seat until Father had to put his hand on her to keep her still. I was glad when finally we reached the Shafers' farm over the hill, brought the horses to a stop in their dooryard, and Father lifted Jessie and me both down. Two little boys were playing there together, lifting rocks into a wooden wagon.

"Hello, Benny," Father said. "Hello, William. How are you boys? Do you like your new babies?"

One boy, busy stacking the rocks in some kind of pattern, ignored him completely. The other scowled and shook his head no.

"Well," said Father, "I'll go in and ask your mother if she'd like to send them back." Laughing, he led Jessie and me to the door, just as it was opened by Mrs. Shafer.

"What are their names?" Jessie asked. "And are they boys or girls? And why don't they have any hair?"

I thought she was rude, but Mrs. Shafer didn't seem to mind. She smiled. "One of each," she said. "No names yet. And as for hair—well, maybe they take after their father."

The two bald babies were both asleep, lying side by side on the kitchen table, where she had placed them for my father to make his examination. Father, opening his bag in the corner of the room, looked over with a smile. "Ben had plenty of hair once, Harriet," he said to Mrs. Shafer. "When we were boys in school together, he had a full head. Curly, if I remember it right.

"I seem to recall that the girls admired that hair quite a bit," he went on, in a teasing voice. "Can't think why he lost it so early. Haven't you been treating him right?"

He turned his attention to the babies, unwrapping the blanket from one and moving its arms and legs gently up and down, bending and unbending them. I watched while he leaned over with his stethoscope and listened to the baby's heart, holding the instrument gently against the tiny chest. I could see the baby's ribs.

I knew enough not to speak while he was listening, but when Father stood back, I whispered to him. "That baby's smaller than Mary was when she was born. They both are."

"Much smaller," he agreed. "Twins usually are. And these two were born early. We feared for them, didn't we, Harriet?"

Mrs. Shafer nodded. "That's why they have no names yet. I didn't want to give names only to see them carved on gravestones."

Father was leaning over the second twin now, looking closely at it, moving its arms and legs, listening to it breathe. I watched as he measured both of their heads. Then carefully he rewrapped them both in their blankets, despite the warm kitchen on this hot July day. He picked them up one at a time, and I could see him thinking as he held them. "They're each more than four pounds, Harriet," he said, after he laid them back down. "Well more. Close to five, I'd say. That many pounds of potatoes would feed your family a good meal, mashed with butter and cream."

"They're eating good," Mrs. Shafer told him.

"I can see that. They're going to make it. Time

to give them names. And you, Harriet? Are you eating? Not working too hard? Does Ben help with the boys?"

"He does. It lets me lie down a bit now and then."

Father looked around the kitchen, at the diapers soaking in a washtub, the pot of something simmering on the wood stove, the broom leaning against the wall in the corner. "Let's put these little no-names back in their cradles, Harriet, and if you come with me into the other room I'll take a listen to your heart as well. Girls? Can we trust you to stay out of mischief? Or maybe you'd like to wash those diapers?"

He was looking at Jessie and me, and I would have been insulted, because he knew I would never be mischievous on a house call. But I understood that he was warning me to keep Jessie out of things. We nodded and agreed to be good, squinching our noses at the mention of the diapers. Then he and Mrs. Shafer each picked up a baby. They seemed as tiny as kittens and just as quiet. Father carried his bag in his other hand and followed Mrs. Shafer down the hall.

"Why does he wear that hat on such a hot day?" Jessie asked me. She wandered around the kitchen, examining the blue and white dishes arranged on a shelf.

"Father? He wears a straw hat. It isn't hot. It

keeps the sun from his eyes. Your father wears one, too. I've seen him."

"No, that boy," Jessie said impatiently. "The one in the field."

"Sit down, Jessie. Don't be touching things."

She flounced herself down in a kitchen chair. "It's not even a farmer's hat. The man had on a straw farmer's hat, but the boy had on that hot old thing. Is he stupid or something?"

She angered me. I didn't want her to be thinking about Jacob, to be asking questions, to be raising doubts. "I don't know," I said curtly. "Look, here's a magazine we can look at." I picked up a ladies' magazine from the cushioned seat of a rocker in the corner and set it in front of Jessie at the table.

Later, though, when we were at home, and alone together, sitting in the parlor after supper while Mother put Mary to bed, I asked Father the same thing. "Why do you think Jacob Stoltz wears that wool cap all the time? Once I saw him take it off at his house, but only because his father forced him."

But Father had no answer. "We all have habits," he said. "Your mother tells me I pull at my ear."

"You do," I told him, "when you're thinking. And Mother chews her lip when she's worried."

"And I recall, Katydid, that when you were very small, you had a pink blanket that you carried everywhere."

"I did? Why don't I remember that?"

133

"You gave it up. It was a baby habit, and you grew to be a girl. But a boy like Jacob—"

"You're pulling your ear, Father."

We both laughed. "Well," he said, "it shows that I'm thinking."

"What about a boy like Jacob?"

"His hat gives him some kind of feeling that he needs to have, is my guess. But since he doesn't talk, we can't ask him what that feeling is. I say he feels a need to hide himself, in a way."

I thought about it, trying to imagine myself with a heavy hat pulled over my hair. "Protect," I said.

"What?"

"A need to protect himself. I think that's what his feeling is."

Father pulled his ear again, then realized it, chuckled, stopped, and grew serious again. "I think you're right, Katy. He protects himself."

"But from what? A hat can't keep you from danger."

"No," Father agreed. "No, it can't. Not physical danger. A falling tree branch would go right through that cap, and Jacob would have himself a fine fractured skull, same as you or me.

"But I think Jacob has his own world inside his head, Katy. I think his cap keeps that world feeling safe."

13. AUGUST 1911

It was August. Hot, still. Mother and I were sitting together on the front porch late on a Tuesday afternoon. Upstairs, Mary was napping; she had been fretful, and we thought she was cutting teeth. Peggy was in the backyard taking the washing from the line. Through the screen door we could hear Naomi in the kitchen, preparing dinner, and through the open window to the parlor, the muffled *slap-slap* of Gram at her card game.

I was just beginning to read *A Girl of the Limberlost* aloud to Mother as she did some needlework. She was embroidering a collar to replace one that had faded, on her blue linen dress.

I would be nine in two months.

I looked up at the end of the first chapter. "I can't understand how *mean* Elnora's mother is," I said. "She doesn't even mind when her own daughter is humiliated in school!"

My own mother smiled. "If she were a perfect mother, the book wouldn't be so interesting," she pointed out.

I thought it over and nodded, because she was right, and I went on to the next chapter.

A late-day breeze lifted the vines growing along the side of the porch. The moonflowers and morning glories shaded the porch, and all summer we had flowers at the beginning and end of the day. The entire neighborhood was shaded by tall elms. Across the street, Mrs. Stevenson was watering the late-blooming rosebushes in her side yard, moving carefully from one to the next, tilting the large spouted can.

Next door, the shades were drawn on the windows of the Bishops' house. Often we drew the shades down to keep the house cool. But the house next door, where Austin lived, had an uncomfortable, inhospitable silence to it. There had been trouble there.

"How quiet it is. The sound of my pages turning

is the only sound," I said to Mother.

But she shook her head and said, "Listen!" And of course then I could hear birds.

"A robin," she said, "with that wonderful throaty song."

"Like gargling," I told her, and we both made a face. Father always makes us gargle with hot salt water for sore throats.

"They'll fly south next month," Mother said. "I always wonder how they—

"Shhh!" she said suddenly. She put down her embroidery hoop and lifted a finger. "What's that?"

We both listened intently. The robin had fallen silent, interrupted by another noise, which seemed to come from the south, toward town, beyond the Methodist church at the corner of the next block. It was a rapid staccato sound, abrupt and ugly, as if some large machinery were starting, stopping, and laboring mightily in between.

Several young boys appeared, running down the middle of the street toward our house, laughing and calling as they looked back. I recognized the Cooper brothers from the next block.

"Here he comes!" one of them called to us. By now several neighbors had come to their porches, and across the street, Mrs. Stevenson had put down her watering can and was watching. From our kitchen, Naomi appeared at the screen door, wiping her hands on her apron, with Gram beside her. Through the open bedroom window I heard Mary stir and whimper upstairs.

The noise had become downright deafening, and then we saw him: Mr. Bishop, Austin's father, grinning with pride, behind the steering mechanism of an automobile as he jounced and sputtered past our house, coming finally to a stop just in front of his own. The machine gave a sort of wheeze, and there was a smoky smell about it. The Cooper brothers had come close and were eyeing it with excitement, curiosity, and fear. From the next block their mother approached, holding a wooden spoon in her hand—she must have been preparing supper. Walking rapidly down from the corner, she called to her boys. "Stand back!" she cried out in alarm. "It might explode!"

Mr. Bishop was wearing goggles. He removed them with a flourish and leapt from the seat of the thing. "You're in no danger," he reassured the Cooper brothers, who hadn't moved an inch, despite their mother's shouted warning. "I'll take the two of you for a spin," he added, and their eyes went wide in delight.

"But first, my wife," he announced. Mrs. Bishop, with Laura Paisley on her hip, had appeared on their porch and was looking with horror at the thing. "Louise?" he called to her proudly. "I have some goggles for you, and a duster!" He held up a garment that was folded beside him on the seat.

"Paul," she called back, "you have taken leave of your senses!"

"*Me,* Father! Take me!" Austin had come from the house now, and down the steps, and was eagerly examining the machine. In a minute Austin was perched beside his father and they were sputtering noisily down the street, while the Cooper boys, wild with envy on the brick sidewalk, looked on. My father, summoned by the commotion, had come from his office with several patients right behind him, and they all stood on the sidewalk, watching.

"Isn't that something!" Father said in an admiring voice. Mrs. Cooper, still holding her spoon, commiserated with Mrs. Bishop and my mother about the extravagant foolishness of men.

The Bishops were the first family in town to own a motorcar, and it cost nine hundred dollars: enough, Peggy said to me as she spooned oatmeal into Mary that evening, to feed a family of orphans for a year.

"I am not at all sure that there can be such a thing as a family of orphans," I told her. "Doesn't a family mean a father and a mother, as well as children? So if the children are orphans, then—"

Peggy frowned at me and I knew enough to

change the subject. Peggy didn't frown often, but her frown was fierce.

"Mr. Bishop says Father should get one. He said it would be an amazing help in case of medical emergencies," I told her. "You know how long it takes for the boy to harness the horses and bring them around. But if he had a Ford automobile, he could simply telephone the garage, and—"

Mary put her hand, suddenly, into the dish of oatmeal and from there into her hair. Peggy sighed and went to the sink to dampen a cloth.

The hall clock struck six. Mother was setting the table for supper. Naomi had made us chicken and corn soup, and there was lovely-smelling fresh-baked bread.

"Katy," Mother said, "go and see if your father will be finished soon." So I scampered away to find him and made the suggestion again as I watched him tidy his office. "So you see, Father, you would simply telephone the garage, and—"

"—and the man at the garage would say, 'I'm so sorry, Dr. Thatcher, I know it's an emergency, but we just can't get the blasted thing started.'"

"Do you think so?"

"I think it's a possiblity. Now those two horses out there—" He pointed through the window to our stable. "They *always* start!"

I giggled. Father was right. We didn't need a Ford motorcar. Neither did the Bishops, really; it was just that Mr. Bishop loved new and astounding things.

Father locked the cabinet where he kept the medicines and put the key back into his pocket. I continued looking through the window toward the stable at the end of our backyard.

"Sometimes Jacob comes to the stable," I told Father suddenly.

"Jacob Stoltz?" Father turned from straightening his desk. He looked surprised. "Levi told me once that he'd seen him looking at our horses."

"Yes. Peggy's brother. He comes a lot. He doesn't hurt anything. He likes the horses."

Father smiled. "He has a horse on his own farm. Maybe he needs to get away from the farm now and then. What he likes is the roaming."

"And me," I pointed out. "I think he likes me. He gave Goldy to me."

"Of course he likes you, Katydid. Everyone does. Come now. Mother's waiting." He locked the office door behind us and we walked around to our front door. On the way, Father said, "The Stoltzes have some trouble in their family, Katy. Maybe you've noticed that Peggy seems upset."

I nodded. I had noticed. "Is it about Nellie?"

"Yes."

I did not understand what had happened. But Nellie had left the Bishops quite suddenly in July. Austin had told me. Austin said that Nellie had packed her things and left, and she was crying. No one would talk about it, not even Peggy. But Nell Stoltz was gone.

"Did she go to New York to be in the pictures, Father? Like Mary Pickford?"

Father frowned. "No, Katy. What ever made you think that? Nellie Stoltz won't ever be in the pictures."

"She wanted to."

"Well, it was a dream she had, perhaps. But she's gone back to the farm."

"But she doesn't like the farm! She never even went to visit!"

Father made an odd snorting sound. "Well, she's visiting there now," he said. "But, Katy? I don't want you to talk about Nell to Mother or to Peggy. They're already upset."

"The Bishops are upset, too. Last week I heard Mr. Bishop shouting at Paul, and then Paul went out the back door and slammed it hard. It woke Mary from her nap, the slam."

"You know," Father said, "it occurs to me that's why his father bought the motorcar: to take their mind off things. Mmmmm. I smell soup."

Father hung his coat in the front hall and we went in to supper. Following him to the table, I wondered what he meant by *things*.

14. SEPTEMBER 1911

G ram had gone back to Cincinnati when summer ended, as she did each year, though this time she said it was harder to go because of Mary. The baby had two teeth in the bottom of her mouth now, and a big, frequent smile. The day before she left, Mr. Bishop set up his camera once again to take a picture of Gram holding Mary. It was next to impossible to make the baby sit still, and at the last minute Laura Paisley insisted on climbing up as well, so that Gram's lap and arms were filled with babies. She said the weight was nothing compared to the joy of it.

School began in September, and my teacher was gray-haired Miss Moody, who sang in the choir at the Presbyterian church so that I saw her on Sundays as well, which seemed strange. Even stranger, Miss Moody had been my mother's third-grade teacher, twenty-five years before! On our very first day of school, Miss Moody looked at me and said, "You are Caro MacPherson's little girl, aren't you?" and for a moment I did not know what she meant. Then I remembered that my mother, though now she was Caroline Thatcher, had once been Caro MacPherson. So I said, "Yes, ma'am" to Miss Moody, and she directed me to what had once been my mother's desk! Imagine, that she had remembered all those years! Even my mother was amazed, when I told her.

Austin, Jessie, and I were all in third grade now. We walked together each morning until we reached the corner where the school was; then Austin went off to be with the boys and to go in the boys' door. Jessie and I walked around to the girls'. The three of us would not be friends again until the end of the day, back in our own neighborhood.

The Bishops had a new hired girl, a sister of Levi's named Flora. She was shy and nervous, not at all playful, which was a disappointment. Nellie had teased a lot and made us all laugh, but Flora did the housework silently, with her head down, and barely spoke. She was good with Laura

Paisley, though, taking her for walks, and I saw them sometimes, hand in hand, and saw that Flora talked then, as if she felt comfortable with someone three years old in a way that she otherwise did not.

I remembered Flora from my school. She had been in sixth grade when I was in first, and I remembered that she had friends then, and gossiped with the other big giggling girls on the playground while we little ones played our recess games of tag and hide-and-seek.

But now Flora had left school to go to work and help her fatherless family.

And someone else had left school as well. Austin's brother, Paul, should have been in his last year of high school this year, but he had gone away. He hadn't wanted to. It was what the shouting, the noisy arguments with his father that I had overheard, had been about. When September came, Paul's things were packed into trunks and then the trunks were lifted into the Ford motorcar and Mr. Bishop drove him to the train station. Their faces were both like stone and they did not speak to each other. On their porch, Mrs. Bishop cried, and Austin waved goodbye. Then Paul went off by train to a boarding school in Connecticut.

"It's a very fine school, Katy," Mother said, when I asked her why Paul had been made to go so far away. "It will prepare him to go to Princeton like his father, and to become a lawyer eventually. Many boys go off to boarding school if their families have the means."

It was a school, she said, only for boys, and I wondered how Paul would feel about that, because he was quite the flirt. I knew he and Nellie had been sweet on each other, but Paul had taken another girl, one from the high school, to the spring cotillion in June, and bought her a camellia corsage. Austin had told me that Paul and the girl won the prize for the Turkey Trot, and Nellie had been very angry when she heard of it, but Paul had laughed at her.

It was the most popular dance. Jessie and I had been practicing it in my room, and we made so much noise that Mother said she was afraid the parlor ceiling would fall down. I thought it served Paul Bishop right to be at a school where there would be no Turkey Trot. Now there would be no girl for him to dance it with, and no Nellie, either, to kiss in the barn and sneer at after.

I wanted a birthday party. Last year, on my eighth birthday, I had been in bed with chicken pox and had opened my gifts in my bedroom, stopping now and then to scratch even though Father kept telling me not to.

Now, about to be nine, looking through the

things stored in the attic, I found our pin-the-tail-on-the-donkey game, the donkey printed on a big oilcloth and punctured with pinholes from other parties. I brought it downstairs and showed Peggy. She had never seen one before.

"You pin it to the wall," I explained, "and then each child has a blindfold on, one after another, and they are spun around in a circle, and then they go to the donkey all blinded, holding a tail, and try to pin it in the right place."

Peggy looked dubiously at the faded donkey I had laid out on the dining room table.

"See how there are pinholes in wrong places? Look! There's a hole in his ear! Jessie Wood did that at my seventh birthday. Then she cried because she didn't win the prize."

"What prize?"

It was surprising to me that Peg knew so little about birthday parties. "The one who gets closest to the tail place gets a prize. At my last party, the one before the chicken pox, the prizes were handkerchiefs for the boys and thimbles for the girls.

"And we do a spider web! Mother will wind string all around, one for each child, and it's like a spider web. You follow your string and at the end you find a surprise! Usually it's just a sweet."

"My land. What else?"

"Oh, games, of course. London Bridge, and Farmer in the Dell. We can do those out in the backyard. And Naomi will make a cake, and there will be ice cream."

Peggy folded the donkey oilcloth carefully and put it in the bottom drawer of the buffet, where the tablecloths were. "It's time to fetch Mary down from her nap," she said.

"Peggy?"

"What?"

"I want to invite Jacob to my birthday party."

She looked at me, astonished. *"Jacob?"*

At that moment my kitten—full-grown now, a good-sized, good-natured cat—hopped down from the chair where he'd been sleeping. He strolled through the room and rubbed himself against my shoe. "He gave Goldy to me," I reminded Peggy.

"Jacob don't go to parties," Peggy said. "He never."

I picked up Goldy, and he hung dangling in my arms like a doll with floppy arms and legs. I listened to his purr. I knew Peggy was right, that it wouldn't do, that Jacob wouldn't understand a party, that the other children would be uneasy if he came.

I told him, though, that I had wanted him to come.

"I'm going to have a birthday party next week, Jacob," I said, when I saw him next. "I wanted to

148

invite you, but Mother said it had to be just children from my class at school.

"I'll be nine," I added.

I wasn't sure that he was even listening, or, if he was listening, whether he understood. He was holding Goldy on his lap, and he stroked the cat's neck with one finger and imitated the purr. We sat side by side on stacked hay in the stable.

"Anyway, I wanted to give you these." I reached into my pocket and pulled out the two big cat's-eye marbles I had brought him. They were both deep brown, flecked with gold and black. I had chosen them from the bag of marbles that Mother had bought at Whittaker's Dry Goods for party prizes and favors. Jacob took them from me and they clicked together in his hand.

He imitated the click with his tongue against his teeth, and smiled in that odd way he had, with his eyes looking someplace else. The horses shifted in their stalls. Goldy yawned and stretched. Outside, a wind came up, and I could hear dead leaves whisper as they broke loose and fell from the branches of the big ash tree in the yard. Our back door opened, and from the kitchen Peggy called me to come in. Jacob looked up at the sound of her voice, and his knees jiggled, but he stayed silent.

15. OCTOBER 1911

I had a new white lawn dress and a huge hair ribbon, and Naomi had made me a cake with buttercream frosting. It was warm enough that Saturday afternoon that Father moved the kitchen table to the backyard and we took the chairs outdoors, too, and set them around the table. Then Mother tied a pink bow on the back of my chair, for my birthday. She laid the table with a yellow cloth and we used my favorite plates, white ones with pink flowers.

I helped to wrap the prizes and watched while Father nailed the oilcloth donkey to the side of the stable. The sun was shining and there were still some chrysanthemums in bloom. Only one thing was wrong. Peggy wasn't there.

Peggy had lived with us now for more than a year, and it felt as if she was part of the family. Mother joked that when Mary began to talk, she would probably call Peggy "Mama."

But today, on my birthday, it was Mother and Naomi who tended Mary, as they had for the past two days. Peggy had been called home for an emergency. Our telephone had rung late two nights before, when I was already in bed, and I heard Father go up to the third floor to get Peggy. Then, after a quick flurry of gathering her things, Father hitched up the horses and took her home.

"She'll be back soon," Mother had reassured me in the morning as I ate my breakfast. The house seemed subdued without Peggy there; she usually bustled about, entertaining Mary, helping me get my things for school, talking to Mother about the plans for the day.

"Will she be here for my party?"

Mother frowned. "I don't think so, Katy. I expect she'll be gone about a week. There's illness in her family, and you know it always takes awhile to heal."

I remembered my own chicken pox and agreed. It takes *forever*.

"Who is ill?"

"I don't know," my mother said.

I guessed that it was Peg's mother who was ill, and I worried for their family because the little girl, Anna, needed a mother. Even with Nellie there, and Peggy, Anna would be frightened if her mother was ill.

I didn't believe it could be Mr. Stoltz, that big strong man who seemed as if nothing could fell him. And I knew it wasn't Jacob. I had seen Jacob just the night before, in our usual place.

He had shown me, pulling them from his pocket, that he carried the two marbles with him. It was odd how Jacob never looked at me—his eyes were always to the side, or his face turned away, and he couldn't, or didn't, ever speak—but he communicated in his own ways. Looking sideways toward the horses, he held out his hand and showed me the marbles; he made the small clicking sound again and nodded his head a little.

"Tomorrow is my birthday party," I told him, "and the boys who come—Austin and Norman and Kenneth—will get marbles. But yours are the best. I chose them out of all the ones we had."

Click. Click. Click.

"The girls—Jessie and Anne are the ones who are coming—will get hair ribbons as favors. I'll get all sorts of gifts, because I'll be the birthday girl," I told him with satisfaction.

Click. Click.

"Peggy's at home, isn't she? And Nellie. I hope things get better there soon. Is it your mother who is ill?"

He returned the marbles to the pocket of his overalls. He was silent now but began to sway slightly, back and forth. His fingers tapped rhythmically on his own knee.

"My baby sister, Mary, was sick last week, with a cough and a fever. But Father gave her medicine and she's all better now. Father says that sometimes *time* is the best healer. But medicine helps, too."

He continued to rock back and forth, seated there on the hay bale.

"And love, of course. My mother says that, and Father says he agrees. When Mary was sick, Mother stayed with her every minute, rocking her, and nursing her, and wiping her forehead with a cool cloth.

"The window right above the kitchen is Mary's window," I said, even as I knew that he would not be interested, "and my room is down the hall, over the porch. My room has blue curtains. You can see them from the yard."

I was just talking aimlessly because I did not know how I could help him. It was clear that Jacob was distressed about something, but it was not something I could understand or make right.

He made a sound and I thought he might be

crying, but I couldn't see his face. Finally, not knowing what to do, I stood up.

"I have to go in now. I have to go to bed early because of the party tomorrow. Mother wants to wash my hair in the morning, and it takes forever to dry."

I tried to think of something less foolish, more helpful, to say.

"I hope things are better in your family soon, Jacob."

Oddly, I wanted to lean forward and kiss the top of his head. It was what both of my parents did when I needed comforting, and it seemed right, somehow, to try to comfort Jacob. But as always he was shielded from the world by the thick cap, and I knew he would recoil from such a touch.

He was a large boy, fourteen by then, with big hands resting on his own knees, and his feet—so often bare, but now, in October, in thick country shoes—almost the size of Father's. I had seen him doing farm chores and knew that he was strong and had a way with animals. Yet he seemed in other ways to be as young and unformed as Mary, with no language but sounds and needs that one could only guess.

Now, in the sunny Indian summer afternoon, the yard was decorated with ribbons and the yellow tablecloth heaped with brightly wrapped gifts. We children played musical chairs, with Father winding the Victrola again and again and Mother removing a chair from the line each time, so that one child would be left out until at the end there would be a winner. The poor old donkey on the stable wall was jabbed again and again, in his nose and tummy and ears, until finally Austin Bishop won the prize by coming close, at least, to where a tail should be.

We went indoors to untangle the spider web that Mother had created with different-colored ribbons and found ourselves crawling under furniture and behind the coat tree to come upon our sweets at the end of each. My cat followed us, leaping again and again to paw at the dangling ribbons, until finally we had to banish poor Goldy to the cellar. Then everyone gathered in the yard to watch me open my presents: embroidered hankies from Jessie, paper dolls, a new skipping rope, a pincushion, and a set of pick-up sticks. Gram had sent a book, *Anne of Green Gables,* from Cincinnati. Finally, Naomi served the cake and ice cream on the table under the ash tree.

The air turned cool after the party guests had gone home. A sudden chilly wind came up, and we hurried to bring in the table and the gifts because it looked like rain was on the way. With so much excitement in the yard that afternoon, and the cake and ice cream, and then the cleaning up to help with after the party guests had gone, I had completely forgotten the strange, sad visit with Peggy's brother the evening before. It was only after my party dress, smeared with cake frosting, was bundled up with the other laundry and I was in my nightgown, sound asleep on a cold rainy night with my new book on the table beside my bed, that Jacob Stoltz reentered my life in a new and terrible way.

The ringing of the telephone woke me in the middle of the night. Or perhaps I was already awake. My memories of that night became confused, afterward, but I believe that something, perhaps the onset of the heavy rainstorm, had woken me earlier. I had heard unfamiliar sounds in the house, which had made me sit up in bed. I listened in the dark, thought I heard a door open and close quietly, thought I heard footsteps on the stairs. There was only silence after that, except for the sound of rain. I decided it had been a dream and drifted off to sleep again. Then, later, the telephone rang.

At our house, we did not have to listen for the rings to make our own combination, the way most others did. Father being a doctor, we had our own line, and the ring was always for us. It was not unusual for the telephone to ring late at night. People seemed to get sickest then, and often Father would have to dress hastily and leave the house, carrying his medical bag, when it was dark and quiet throughout the town.

So I was not surprised by the ringing of the telephone, or hearing Father's feet on the stairs as he went down to answer it, or his murmured voice to Mother as he dressed in the night. I snuggled back again into my pillow, imagining him hurrying to the hospital, probably, only two streets away. Maybe he would not even take the buggy. He would walk quickly, carrying his bag. In the morning, at breakfast, he would tell us of a sudden illness and a family stricken with fear. Once it had been a small child: meningitis, Father had said, but she would get well. Once an old man we knew slightly from church: his heart, it was, and he would not recover. We watched the funeral procession go from the church to the cemetery a few days later.

But on the night of my birthday, it was different. As I lay there half-awake, I became aware of other, more unusual sounds. I heard my father go to the telephone again, and when he spoke to the operator I recognized the number that he gave her: 426. He was calling the Bishops' house, next door. Through my slightly opened bedroom window, even through the rain, I could actually hear their telephone ring; and after a moment I saw lights go on in their parlor, and I knew Mr. Bishop had risen, as my father had, to answer it.

I heard my father speak, though I could not make out the words. Then he left the house and I saw him move through the rain across the yard toward the Bishops'. I saw the two men meet on the porch and talk. While I watched they went to the barn, where Mr. Bishop kept the Ford motorcar, and then I heard—I'm sure the whole neighborhood heard—the sound as he cranked the motor to a start and in a moment, the loud sputter and rattle as it moved from the barn to the alley, then the street, and off. I had thought Father was in the car with Mr. Bishop, but after a moment I could I hear sounds in our stable and I knew Father was hitching Jed and Dahlia. Then he, too, was gone, in the buggy.

The night had turned very cold, and the rain had become a windy downpour. Indian summer was over. Shivering in my thin nightgown, I pulled the bedroom window closed and went to ask Mother what was happening.

"There's trouble at the Stoltz farm" was all she would say. "They need help."

She let me climb into the big bed, on Father's side. We lay there side by side, her arm around me, her hand stroking my hair. After a while, I slept.

It was light when Mother stirred and sat up. I opened my eyes.

"Is Father home?"

"No, not yet. Try to sleep some more. It's very early. I'm just going to feed Mary." She rose from the bed and put on her blue dressing gown, which had been draped over a chair.

Then I heard my baby sister making her cheerful early-morning sounds—laughing and gurgling—from the nursery down the hall. Mary was six months old now and slept all night, a great blessing, for there had been times when she was younger and Mother had had to go to her again and again.

I lay snuggled in the warm cocoon of my parents' bed and listened to Mother move down the hall, open Mary's door, and speak softly to the baby. The sounds were familiar, though most often I slept through the ritual. Mother would lift her from the crib, change her wet diaper, wrap her in her pink blanket, and sit in the upholstered rocking chair while Mary nursed.

But on this ruined dawn, the sleepy ceremony of sounds was interrupted by Mother's terrible cry.

In a moment she was back, holding Mary in her arms. She thrust the baby and a clean diaper at me, and said, "Watch Mary. Change her. Don't let her fall off the bed."

Mother's face was white. She took several deep breaths. "Katy? Are you awake? Are you paying attention? I have to go use the telephone. Take care of Mary. And do not go into the nursery. Do you hear me?"

I nodded. I laid the baby on her back beside me, and she grabbed at the sheet with her chubby hands.

"Promise me! Stay out of the baby's room."

"I promise." Mary was wiggling, and I held a corner of her nightie tightly so that she wouldn't make her way to the edge of the high, wide bed and fall.

Mother hurried from the bedroom and down the stairs to the telephone in the front hall. Obediently I unpinned Mary's wet diaper and began to fold the dry one into some sort of shape that I could pin around her. I had watched Mother and Peggy do it often enough, but it seemed very complicated now that I tried it on my own. Below, I could hear Mother's voice, but I couldn't hear what she was saying because Mary had begun to whimper. When I finally had the diaper secured as best I could, I picked her up and carried her downstairs just as Mother hung up the telephone.

"She's hungry." I handed her, crying loudly now, to Mother.

"Father's coming," she said tersely. She went to a chair in the parlor and sat down to feed Mary.

"I thought he was at the Stoltzes'."

"He was. I called there. He's coming home." She stroked Mary's fine hair. The baby was quiet now, nursing.

"What's wrong, Mother?"

But she only shook her head. "Katy, you know the Stoltz boy; what's his name? Joseph?"

"Jacob."

"Yes, Jacob. I should have remembered. Your father just said it."

"Did something happen to him?"

"No. But Peggy said you had become a sort of friend to him." Mother gave an odd laugh. "She told me you wanted to invite him to your birthday party.

"Was that just yesterday?" she asked suddenly. "It seems so long ago." She lifted Mary to her shoulder and began to pat her back. "Get a rag, Katy, in case she spits."

I went to the kitchen and brought her a clean cloth from the place where Naomi kept them folded. Gently Mother wiped some milky bubbles from Mary's mouth.

"What about Jacob?"

"They're looking for him. He seems to have run off. Your father said to ask you if you know where he might have gone."

"He goes everywhere. He roams." Even as I said it, I knew where I would look for him. "I'm cold,

Mother. I'm going to go get dressed."

Mother bit her lip. "No, I think you should stay down—" Then she looked at my bare feet and my thin nightgown. I was hugging my arms around me.

"All right," she said. "Run up and put on some warm clothes. But come right back down. And don't—"

"I already promised, Mother. I won't go into Mary's room."

When I came downstairs, Mary was wrapped in an afghan and asleep on a corner of the parlor sofa with a chair pulled up beside so that if she rolled she wouldn't fall. I had dressed hastily and needed help with the back buttons of my brown plaid dress. Mother was in the kitchen, and I could hear Naomi's voice. Naomi always arrived early in the morning, even on rainy Sundays like this.

I went into the kitchen, needing to be where there was warmth.

"A whole group has gone out Lawton County Road, looking. I saw them gathered at the police station when I walked past," Naomi was telling Mother. Mother nodded distractedly and began to set some places at the kitchen table. Father would be hungry when he came in. I could tell from the way Naomi talked, excited but not especially alarmed, that she did not know the whole of it, that she simply thought the touched boy had run off and needed finding before he caught pneumonia from the rain.

When the table was set, I stood with my back to Mother while she did my buttons.

"I recollect when those Cooper boys got lost out near Fielder's Pond. They'd gone looking for frogs and wandered too far. My land, they was just little things, then. Maybe five and six?" Naomi began to slice bread. She chattered on and didn't seem to notice that Mother was silent and tense, not listening to her.

I felt her fingers fumbling at the back of my dress and perceived her silence as that of a person stunned. I felt the same way, now, speechless and paralyzed. I had obeyed Mother. I had not gone into Mary's room. But the door had been open a crack, and I had pushed it open further and peeked. I knew, now, what she had seen there, because I had seen it, too.

16. OCTOBER 1911

Father came in through the back door with another man, their clothes dripping. He had left the buggy standing in the driveway, the horses there in the rain; it was unusual for him to do that. They should have been taken to the stable and rubbed down. He should be calling Levi to come and tend them, to rub them down and give them oats.

But the horses stood silent in the rain, and Father ignored Naomi's offer of hot coffee and a dry cloth to wipe his face and hands. He looked at Mother and she rose and took him silently to the stairs. The other man followed. I began to go with them, but Mother spoke sharply to me from the landing.

"Stay downstairs," she said. Then she felt something under her foot. Leaning down, she picked it up and handed it impatiently to me. "Put this away, Katy. It's left from your party."

I took it from her, knowing she was mistaken, but said nothing. I put it into my pocket.

I heard their voices upstairs, moving down the hall toward Mary's room. I knew what they would see there and wondered what they would do. It didn't seem to matter much. Nothing did. Except, perhaps, Jacob.

I checked the baby, who was still sleeping soundly on the parlor sofa, her small hands outstretched. Then I pulled on a heavy jacket from the hall closet, and when Naomi was turned toward the stove and didn't see me slip through the kitchen, I let myself out the back door and ran through the rain to the stable.

I found him there, huddled behind the hay bales, in the corner where I had once come upon Nellie and Paul, near the shelf where the can of harness oil was kept, and beside the covered barrel of oats and the bridles and harness hung from hooks on the wall. He was half-asleep but shivering, his clothes very wet. I knew he had been there for hours. He must have been alarmed when Father entered in the night and moved the horses out. Knowing his way of being, I thought that he had probably been sitting close to the horses and then had run to hide when he heard Father come.

He clutched the handle of a rake as if he might have need of a weapon.

"Here," I said to him, and held the gold-flecked brown marble out. "You dropped this on our stairs."

He released the rake, took the marble from me, put it into his pocket where it clicked against the other, and looked at the floor. His shoulders were hunched, and he still shivered with cold. I went and got a horse blanket from where it hung folded over the door of the stall. I draped it over Jacob's shoulders.

We sat silently together there in the stable, and I sorted out a clear picture of what had happened. Slowly I said it all to Jacob, knowing he would not respond, but the saying of it fixed it firmly in my mind, and I knew I would have to explain it soon to the others.

"Nellie had a baby, didn't she? And she didn't want it. It was born but she wouldn't take it, wouldn't feed it."

He was silent.

I could picture the cold bedroom of the little farmhouse. Probably they had moved Anna to her parents' room again when Nellie went home in disgrace. And for the past two days Peggy had been there, too, to help. I pictured the family gathered there in anguish while Nellie gave birth to a baby who came unwanted into the world.

"Did it come early, Jacob? It was very small. Much smaller than Mary was when she was born, and even smaller than the Shafers' twins.

"Was it born alive? I know some aren't."

He made a sound, then, and at first I thought he was imitating the sound of a kitten, something I had heard him do in the past. But he made the mewing sound again, and I knew, suddenly, that it was the sound of the newborn baby.

I touched his shoulders through the thick plaid blanket and he did not pull away. "It was like the kittens, wasn't it? You used to take the new kittens down to the creek. Peggy told me. She said you were gentle with them. Did you do that to the baby, Jacob?"

He cried out then, harshly, and pulled his shoulders away from my hand.

The door to the stable opened, and my father was standing there. "Katy," he said to me, "I have to take the boy in now."

I stood in front of Jacob as if to shield him. "He meant no harm, Father!"

"The court will decide."

I could feel Jacob's fear behind me, and with it something else. Anger. He had responded with that harsh, angry cry when I talked about the kittens. Suddenly I became aware of what had happened.

"Father!" I said. "I need to know—"

"Katy, a terrible thing has happened that you know nothing about," Father said in a stern voice. "I must take the boy *now*."

"But I do know, Father! I saw it! I looked into Mary's room and saw it! The red hair made me know it was Nellie's," I said, whispering it, explaining it to myself.

"And it was wet. But, Father, I need to know this: was the *baby* wet, or was it just the feed sack, from the rain?"

Father looked at me, puzzled, and I think saddened that I had seen. "The baby's body was dry," he said.

I turned back to Jacob. "I'm sorry," I told him. "I was wrong, Jacob. It was like the lamb, wasn't it? Its mother turned away, but you found a better mother who already had a baby of her own so she could feed it. Remember? I saw it in your barn, the day you gave Goldy to me."

I thought of that lamb, as fleecy as a child's toy, comfortable in the pen beside the mother that Jacob had found to save its life. Alive, fed, the lamb bore no resemblance to the limp, gray, staring thing wrapped in the wet feed sack that I had glimpsed in Mary's crib. But Jacob had meant only to save Nellie's baby by bringing it to my mother. I was certain of that. It was just too small, and the night too cold and wet; the journey was too long.

Outside, behind Father, through the rain, I heard heavy feet on the back steps. More men had arrived and were entering our house. I knew there was very little time left. I turned back to Jacob.

"You must come now, Jacob," I told him. "They're looking for you." I lifted the blanket from him and helped him stand. Though he had always withdrawn from my touch in the past, now he let me hold his hand and take him to the house, where the men were waiting. My father led the way.

"Father," I called, as they took Jacob away, "don't let them take his cap."

I never saw the touched boy again. The court determined that he should be confined to the Asylum at the edge of town, and I thought of him there in that many-windowed stone building where people screamed or sat silent. I hoped that they would let him roam outdoors, though I think I knew they would not. I hoped he would be given a kitten, though I knew he would not.

He was fourteen then. It was 1911. Nearly fifty years later the Asylum closed its doors. The remaining patients, subdued by new medications, returned to their families or were moved to other places. But his name appeared on no list that I ever saw, and there seemed to be no record by then of a Jacob Stoltz. Perhaps in long-ago discarded papers one could have found some mention of him, proof that he had existed, that he had loved animals and had once tried to save an unnamed baby but had failed.

17. PAUL, AFTER

Paul Bishop rarely returned to the house where he had spent his early years, grown to manhood, and fathered a child. He graduated from a Connecticut boarding school and went on to Princeton as his parents had hoped, and from there to law school, where he spent two and a half restless, dissatisfied years.

When he was twenty-three and war was raging in Europe, Paul Bishop left law school against his parents' wishes and enlisted in the U.S. Marines. He came home after his basic training to say goodbye to his family before he left for France, but it was a harsh parting shadowed with blame and anger.

Austin and I were in our teens by then, and our childhood friendship had turned into the shy beginning of something more. We sat together on the front porch and watched while Mr. Bishop set up his camera. Paul's mother came from the house and stood beside her husband's newest automobile. Her son, wearing a uniform and high brown boots, stood stiff and awkward as a stranger on her other side, and they did not move close enough to touch. The brim of Paul's hat shaded his eyes. At the last moment Laura Paisley ran forward and handed her new puppy to her mother.

Mr. Bishop fiddled with his camera and then ordered them to smile, but they appeared unable. I remember that Peggy, who would be leaving us soon, watched through the parlor window of our house, and I could not put a name to the look on her face.

On June 5, 1918, Lieutenant Bishop of the 4th Marine Brigade died in battle at a place called Belleau Wood, fifty miles from Paris.

18. NELL, AFTER

No one, not even her family, ever really knew where Nellie went when she left the farm soon after that October night. For years I looked for her in the movies, reading the lists of minor characters, searching for her name or for the name Evangeline Emerson, which she had chosen once as more glamorous than her own.

Someone, a friend of my father's, once thought he saw her in Baltimore, working in a tavern. At least, he said, it was a plump, red-headed woman with a loud laugh and a tired look, and she was known to everyone as Nellie. We wondered whether to tell Peggy. But we decided that it would be cruel, so we kept silent.

19. PEGGY, AFTER

Peg stayed with us until Mary started school. Then, when she was twenty-one years old, she went back home and married Floyd Lehman, the farmhand who had waited all those years. We attended their wedding at the country church and gave them a gift of gold-rimmed dishes like those she had loved at our house.

Eventually Peggy and Floyd took over the Stoltz farm, added rooms and plumbing to the house, and lived there with their three little girls and Peggy's parents. Pup lived on there, too, until he was seventeen years old, and for all those years he lifted his head, waiting, each time the door opened, as if someone he had lost might be returning.

20. SCHUYLER'S MILL, AFTER

The ruins of the burned mill remained untouched for many years. When Austin and I were married, in 1928, his parents and mine, together, bought the property and gave it to us as a wedding gift. It took us two years to turn it into a home. By then automobiles were no longer a novelty but an everyday reality, and the road, once dirt, had been paved. It was easy for me to live out in the countryside, a short trip by car to the hospital if I was called in for an emergency.

Our children grew up here, went away when they were grown, and brought their own little ones here to visit. Now the grandchildren bring theirs. Until his death last year, Austin, a historian, sat every day in his office, writing, and looked out at the creek rushing past. He said it helped him think.

I still hear it at night, the tumble and foam of the water, and sometimes, in my memory, I can hear the *shoooda, shoooda, shoooda* of the great grindstone and I picture the touched boy standing there, watching.